HOPE IN THE HOLLER

Also by Lisa Lewis Tyre

Last in a Long Line of Rebels

HOPE
IN THE
HOLLER

LISA LEWIS TYRE

 NANCY PAULSEN BOOKS

NANCY PAULSEN BOOKS
an imprint of Penguin Random House LLC
375 Hudson Street
New York, NY 10014

Library of Congress Cataloging-in-Publication Data
Names: Tyre, Lisa Lewis, author.
Title: Hope in the holler / Lisa Lewis Tyre.
Description: New York, NY : Nancy Paulsen Books, [2018]
Summary: Upon her mother's death, Wavie Conley, eleven, must go live
with a scheming aunt in the Kentucky town her mother left behind.
Identifiers: LCCN 2017033535 | ISBN 9780399546310 (hardcover) | ISBN 9780399546334 (ebook)
Subjects: | CYAC: Orphans—Fiction. | Grief—Fiction. | Friendship—Fiction. | Aunts—Fiction. |
Adoption—Fiction. | Family life—Kentucky—Fiction. | Kentucky—Fiction. | BISAC:
JUVENILE FICTION / Family / Parents. | JUVENILE FICTION / Social Issues / Death & Dying. |
JUVENILE FICTION / Social Issues / Emotions & Feelings.
Classification: LCC PZ7.1.T97 Hop 2018 | DDC [Fic]—dc23
LC record available at https://lccn.loc.gov/2017033535

Printed in the United States of America.
ISBN 9780399546310
1 3 5 7 9 10 8 6 4 2

Design by Jaclyn Reyes.
Text set in Tactile ITC Std, AdPro LT Std, and Flyerfonts.

For Rachel

CHAPTER ONE

An actual clown conducted my mama's funeral. He didn't wear clown clothes, or greasepaint, but I'd read his biography on the Andro Funeral Home website, which had included his hobby along with the facts that he'd been married for thirteen years and had a son named Angus.

Mama had been especially tickled. "They ought to change their tagline to *We Put the 'Fun' in Funerals!*"

"Sounds like your funeral will be a real three-ring circus," I said.

"Write it down, Wavie," she'd answered. "I want my pallbearers to ride in on unicycles." When she laughed, I giggled along with her even though I didn't find planning the funeral one bit funny. But when your mama is practically face-to-face with the Grim Reaper, you do what you can.

It had been Mama's idea, fueled by our long hours waiting in hospital rooms and the need to find something else to think about: to take words and see how many new ones we could make out of the letters. "Doesn't cost but two cents' of graphite, Wavie. Try it!"

There are all sorts of words to make out of F-U-N-E-R-A-L. FUN, of course, and LUNAR, LEAF and EARFUL. There were ninety-six if you counted words that people use for Scrabble but aren't really words, like NU and ER. My favorite was UNREAL. That's a perfect word to describe the day you lay your mama to rest.

In the end, there hadn't been any unicycles, or even pallbearers for that matter. Mama had left instructions to be cremated with only a small graveside service for the burial of her ashes, conducted by the part-time clown.

I slipped my hand into the pocket of my dress and felt the corner of the Andro Hospital stationery with the list Mama had made for me. I'd memorized it, but I liked being able to look at her handwriting.

It was seven final instructions.

1. Use Andro's. A man that moonlights as a clown and names his son after a steak sounds like someone I'd like to know.

2. I left a cutting from our peony bush in a pot by the front door. Peonies are fickle, so don't plant it until you're sure you're staying put somewhere. It was from my mama's plant and she grew the prettiest peonies in Kentucky. You can look at it and know I'm with you in spirit.

3. The chaplain said since I'm a believer, you and I would meet in heaven if you act right. I told him if it depended on how we acted, it'd be a right lonely place. Just 'cause someone's in charge don't mean they're smart. Think for yourself. Also, be good. It doesn't hurt to cover all your bases.

4. No dropping out of school! I'm banking on you being the first Conley to ever go to college. U-N-I-V-E-R-S-I-T-Y even has some fine words in it like NURSE and VET!

5. Cry when you need to but don't dwell. It won't bring me back and you've got to get on with living.

6. Be brave, Wavie B.! You got as much right to a good life as anybody, so find it!

7. Never, ever forget that I loved being your mama more than anything in this big, wide world.

She'd signed it *xoxo, Mama.*

I'd already heard most everything on the list, except the part about my grandmother's peonies. Mama hardly ever talked about her family and she hadn't gone back to her hometown since my grandmother died. *I parted ways with the rest of them right after you were born and as far as I'm concerned it was a good trade. It's just you and me, Wavie, against the world. Sounds like a fair fight to me!*

My eyes stung and the cemetery blurred. Now it was just me. Wavie against the world didn't have the same ring to it. I blinked twice, willing the tears back into my eyeballs. If I started crying now, I was afraid I'd never stop, and making a scene at Mama's graveside service would really have the neighbors at Castle Fields Mobile Home Park talking.

I focused on the weather instead. The man on TV had said to expect spring showers, but so far the rain had held off. The wind was starting to pick up, though, and had blown a fistful of dirt from the mound by Mama's urn across the scuffed dress shoes of my best friend, Hannah, and the black slip-ons of her granny Mrs. Watkins.

There was only a small cluster of folks attending, mostly neighbors from our mobile home park, but I spotted a few other faces in the back—Mrs. Leslie, Mama's old boss from Walmart; a nurse from the oncology floor; my math teacher, Mr. Stephens; and a few classmates. Everyone wore black, and we stood there hunched against the cold breeze like crows on a wire trying to decide where to fly next.

A beat-up sedan drove through the gates and parked down the hill, its brakes squeaking. Two people sat inside watching us, but they didn't get out. It wasn't a friendly-looking car. Mama said you can't judge a book by its cover, but I think sometimes you can. I mean, one look at *Harry Potter* and I knew it was going to be about magic. That B-U-I-C-K (BUCK, ICK) car was dented and banged up like it was mad at the world and ready to run down whatever got in its way.

My caseworker, Mrs. Chipman, patted my shoulder as the funeral director placed the biodegradable urn into a small hole in front of a plaque that read simply, *Ronelda May Conley, Beloved Mother.* A few people came up and hugged me, muttering things like, "She was a fine woman," and "She'll be missed," until Mrs. Chipman nodded that I could go and sit in her car.

I could feel the stares of the people as they walked by, and could imagine their conversations as they got into their cars. *Poor kid. Orphaned at eleven, how pitiful.* I leaned my head forward until it hit my knees, and closed my eyes.

Someone tapped softly on the glass. "Wavie, are you all right?"

I sat back up and rolled down the window.

"Hey, Hannah." I put my hand out the window and laced my fingers through hers.

She wiped her eyes with her free hand. "I am so, so sorry."

I nodded.

Hannah dug an envelope out of her pocket and handed it through the window. "The trailer park took up a collection. It's not much, but hopefully it'll help."

The envelope was heavy and I could feel an abundance of change. It was all I could do to choke out an answer. "Tell everybody I said thanks."

Hannah gave me a final sad smile and turned to leave.

The driver's side door opened and Mrs. Chipman settled into the front seat. Then she reached back and rubbed my shoulder. "You ready?"

I looked once more toward the grave site. "Yes."

Everyone was gone except for the old car I'd noticed earlier. As we moved to pass it, the driver held up a hand for us to stop.

We watched as a woman with long, frizzy blond hair got out and walked toward us. A grumpy-looking teenager stayed in the car, slumped against the window.

"Why is that woman dressed like a cat?" I asked.

"That's called leopard print," Mrs. Chipman said.

Leopard Lady was top-heavy, with broad shoulders and skinny legs. She wore leopard-print leggings under a leopard-print sweater.

When she got to the car, she motioned for Mrs. Chipman to open the window, then bent down and stared into the backseat.

"Wavie? Wavie Conley? Is that you?"

I leaned back against the seat. "Yes?"

"Why, I'm your aunt, Samantha Rose! I've come to take care of you."

See. *UNREAL*.

CHAPTER TWO

Everything about Leopard Lady was loud—her bright, bleached hair, the bracelets that jangled when she moved her arms, and especially her voice. Half of Castle Fields was probably outside our trailer, listening to our business.

She sat sprawled in Mama's chair. It looked so wrong that I felt my heart start to sink, weighted down, into my body. Like that time the Baptists held a free dental clinic and they put a heavy apron-thing on me so I wouldn't get radiation poisoning. They ought to make an apron to guard against people poisoning.

"I swear, Hoyt, she looks just like her mama!"

"Sure. Whatever." His hair covered the top half of his face as he stared down at his phone. All I could see was the lower half—a small mouth, an even smaller wisp of a mustache, and a smattering of chin acne. I wasn't usually bad tempered but I wanted nothing more than to punch the sullen look off his pimpled face. No matter what had gone wrong with his day, burying his mama wasn't on the list.

"I'm Samantha Rose, honey, the older sister of your departed mother. This here's your cousin Hoyt." She dabbed at her eyes with a tissue. "I can't believe we have to meet under these terrible circumstances." She stood up and grabbed me in a big bear hug.

My head was smashed into the leopard bosom and I got a nose full of onions and stale smoke before Mrs. Chipman cleared her throat and Samantha Rose released me.

"Wavie, have a seat." Mrs. Chipman motioned me toward the couch and waited until I was perched on its edge. "So it seems like your aunt has made a request for guardianship. Isn't that good news?"

I pulled the list out of my pocket and laid it on my lap. "Mama didn't mention anything about an aunt on this."

"What's that?" Samantha Rose asked. She held out her beefy hand. "Can I read it?"

I couldn't see a way to refuse, so I handed it over.

Samantha Rose's lips moved as she read. "Well. Right here it mentions my mama's flowers. If that don't tell you she was longing for her family I don't know what would."

"Maybe a line saying she was longing for her family?" I asked. Sometimes you've got to point out the obvious.

Samantha Rose frowned, but I kept going. "Why didn't Mama mention having a sister before?" I asked Mrs. Chipman. "When she filled out the paperwork?" For all we knew this woman was a crazy child abductor who trolled cemeteries.

"Wavie's right. Our first priority when finding a home for children is to place them with family," Mrs. Chipman said. "We asked Ronelda if she had relatives and she said there was no one."

Samantha Rose folded the note carefully and handed it back. "Unfortunately me and Ronelda had a falling-out a few years ago. She probably figured we wouldn't help. And now it's too late to make up with her and say all the things I wanted to say to my little sister." She blew her nose with a loud honk. "But I *can* make it up to her. I can take care of her sweet baby girl."

Mrs. Chipman's cell phone rang. "Excuse me. This will be the office."

Samantha Rose stared at me through lashes thick with mascara. For somebody who'd been so upset, she didn't have any black streaks on her cheeks to show for it.

"It's like seeing a young Ronelda again. That reminds me." She picked up a hot-pink purse the size of a toaster oven from the floor near her feet and plopped it into her lap. After a few seconds of searching, she handed me a photo album.

It was small and plastic with the word *Photo* written in fancy script on the front. I opened the cover and sure enough, there was Mama's face staring back. Young, younger even than I was now, but it was her. I flipped through the pictures. Mama as a toddler in a blow-up swimming pool, Mama in a faded sundress drinking an Ale-8 on a front porch, a teenage Mama with her hair in a ponytail holding a fishing rod and a tiny fish. I dropped the album onto the couch beside me, dizzy. There was a whole life between those plastic covers that I'd never known existed.

"I think she's gonna pass out," Hoyt said. "Cool!"

"Hoyt, shut your piehole." Samantha Rose leaned forward in the chair and patted my knee. "You'll be okay, sugar. It just takes some getting used to, I know."

Mrs. Chipman walked back into the room. "Everything seems to check out, Wavie. Your aunt and uncle were approved as temporary guardians for you this morning." She smiled like she'd just delivered great news; I could practically see the relief coming off her in waves—problem solved.

The problem of course had been what to do with me. I hadn't liked it when Mama talked about what would happen if she died, but she'd insisted on being prepared. Hannah and her granny had been plan A. Mrs. Watkins had agreed to be my guardian, but then two weeks before Mama died, Hannah's own mother had shown up with an old boyfriend and a new baby. There wasn't room for another mouth to feed in their small trailer and Mama was gone before she could make a plan B.

"I'm going with them?"

"Yes, I've been instructed to release you to your family for the time being." She smiled. "But I'll be in touch soon to make sure this is a suitable arrangement."

Mrs. Chipman and Samantha Rose talked, ironing out all the details. I flipped through the photo album again, looking at Mama's face. It wasn't until the third time through that I noticed Samantha Rose. She was in the background of a bunch of the pictures and she wasn't smiling in a single one. In fact, she was mostly glaring—at my mom.

CHAPTER THREE

Samantha Rose didn't look or sound a thing like Mama. Mama had been tall and thin, and Leopard Lady wasn't. Mama had dark hair and blue eyes, while Samantha Rose's hair was yellow blond, and her eyes were brown. When Mama talked, her tone was soft and sweet. Samantha Rose sounded like a twangy banjo with a broke string. Maybe if she'd been at all like Mama, I'd have been more excited at the prospect of an aunt. If Mama had even hinted at having a sister somewhere, it might have felt real, but she hadn't.

I wasn't sure how I'd gone from being an orphan to having a new family in the space of an hour, but I didn't like it. Of course, I didn't like anything at the moment. I admit that burying my mama's ashes an hour earlier might have warped my perspective.

The walls of my room were thin as watery soup and I could hear Samantha Rose and Hoyt down the hall going through Mama's things. All of it had been put into boxes already. There was only four days left before rent was due and Mr. Randolph wouldn't wait on anybody, no sirree, Bob. He wasn't running a homeless shelter. Mrs. Chipman had wanted to call the thrift store and schedule a pickup, but I'd convinced her to leave everything for the neighbors to go through after the funeral.

Stuffed in my old backpack by the door were two pairs of pants, three T-shirts, three sets of underwear, my toothbrush, all the photos I owned, my school yearbook, my notepad and a dog-eared New Testament that Mama had kept by her bed. All my worldly possessions, not including the peony, were in one bag. I pulled a photo of me and Mama from the front pocket and propped it up beside me.

I reached over and turned the shade to block the afternoon sun. I was worn out and all I wanted to do was go to sleep and never move again. The hospital had sent a counselor to talk to me about grief, but he fell a little short in describing it to me. He should have just hit me with a Taser. I imagined it would feel about the same.

The absence of Mama was everywhere. I could feel her *not* in the trailer, *not* in my room, *not* anywhere. *Not.*

Mama had been sick for a long time. Those last few days were the worst, but she'd done everything she could to prepare me for her leaving.

I know it's going to be hard, but you can do it, she'd whispered. *I have faith in you. Whenever you get to feeling blue, think about a happy time when we were together having fun.*

What good will that do? I asked.

I don't know. Maybe heaven works likes television shows. Did you know that every time a rerun airs on TV, the actors get a check in the mail? It's called a royalty payment.

I shook my head. *Every single time?*

That's right. Maybe when you think about something we did together, I'll get my own kind of royalty payment. She leaned her head back against the pillows, smiling. *I'll be in heaven smiling and laughing with you.*

It was worth a shot. I closed my eyes and thought about a day when we'd gone to Adventure Cove, a local amusement park. It was one of my happiest memories. Mama had a hat on that hid her baldness and she'd put on a little bit of weight. If you didn't know any better, she almost looked healthy. She sat on a bench eating popcorn and watched while I rode the Flying Swings over and over.

I tried to concentrate on how Mama had looked that day, but it was no use. The sugary smile of Samantha Rose kept floating through my head. I sniffed. I could smell the smoke all the way back in my room. Mama hadn't smoked at all and she'd gotten cancer anyway. I inhaled a deep breath and held it, imagining the carcinogens diving down into my lungs and latching on to my blood cells. Dying wasn't scary anymore. Living was.

The letters M - E - L - A - N - O - M - A floated against my eyelids. MEAN, ALONE and MOAN. Nothing good could ever be made out of that word. My eyes were squeezed as tight as I could make them, but I couldn't stop a tear from working its way out and running down my face.

I'd taken Mama's blanket off her bed when she went to the hospital for the last time and I wrapped it around me now, breathing in the scent of her. The thought of never seeing Mama again, of not being able to ask her all the questions that were racing through my head, was too much. I buried my head into the blanket folds and cried myself to sleep.

A BRIEF KNOCK sounded on the door, then Samantha Rose poked her head through. "Up and at 'em, lazybones. You want something to eat before we get on the road? It's a good two hours and I don't plan on stopping."

I sat up, groggy and confused. "What? It's morning already?"

"Yep, and somebody just dropped off biscuits."

"That'd be Mrs. Florence. She makes biscuits whenever something bad happens." I wiped the sleep from my eyes and glanced at my plastic wristwatch. I'd slept seventeen hours straight and if Samantha Rose would've left and closed the door, I could've probably slept for seventeen more.

"Huh. You'd think she'd be better at it, then; these are half-burnt." She opened the door wider and leaned up against the doorjamb.

"You're wearing Mama's robe," I whispered.

"I didn't figure Ro needed it anymore." She ran a hand down the pink, fluffy lapel. It was too small and gaped in the middle, exposing her pajamas. "Better me than one of these scavengers watching out their trailer windows for us to leave."

Scavengers? It took me a second to realize she was talking about the neighbors, the same people that had checked in on me those nights when Mama was too weak to cook supper. Our friends, like Hannah and her granny. I stared at the worn carpet in my bedroom. Anything was better than looking at this stranger in Mama's housecoat. "I'm not hungry."

Samantha Rose nodded. "Suit yourself." She looked around the room. "Ronelda couldn't wait to see her hometown in her rearview mirror, and look where she ended up. Different trailer park, same old story."

"Why didn't she like it there?"

"Thought she was too good for us, I guess." Samantha Rose shrugged.

I remembered the photographs of the two of them. "Do you still live where you and Mama grew up?"

"Yup." She felt around the pockets of the robe and fished out a cigarette. "Right where we was reared in Conley Holler—named after our pa, Hap Conley, a man meaner than a skillet full of rattlesnakes." She said it like she was proud of the fact. "It's just on the other side of the mountain."

She gestured toward the desk. "What's that?"

I'd forgotten about the envelope of cash Hannah had given me. "The trailer park took up a collection."

Samantha Rose picked up the envelope and began counting. "Twenty-three dollars and fourteen cents?" she said out of the corner of her mouth. "That's it? That's the best they could do?"

"Yeah, that's it," I repeated in a low voice. "It's too bad they have to hoard their money for silly stuff, like food and electricity."

She gave me a dirty look and tucked the envelope into her pocket. "Well, this'll pay for the gas getting back, anyway. Get your things together. We're gonna head home."

Home. Mama's home, a place she'd left and barely mentioned. I picked up the picture of her and stuffed it into the backpack. A whole life of stories she could have told, but obviously didn't want to, and now never would.

The *not* of Mama kept growing.

CHAPTER FOUR

I sat in the backseat of the Buick as we drove out of Castle Fields Mobile Home Park and onto the highway. My backpack was at my feet, Mama's blanket was folded on my lap and the potted peony sat beside me, held in place with its own seat belt.

The trees lining the side of the road blurred into a sea of green as we sped past. Goodbye, Hannah. Goodbye, Mr. Stephens and the Andro sixth-grade class. Goodbye, life with Mama.

You got as much right to a good life as anybody, so find it, Mama had written on the list.

It was the central theme of our final conversations. *Ain't nobody any better than you, Wavie Boncil. The good Lord says everybody has a hope and a future.* I rubbed the back of my hand across her blanket. I'd hoped that Mama would get well and that hadn't turned out. Where was her future?

"Ronelda only came back to the Holler once, back when Mama died," Samantha Rose said from the front seat. "But now you're coming back and gonna be right where you belong."

"Is it just you and Hoyt?" I asked.

"And your uncle." Samantha Rose adjusted the rearview mirror so she could look at me. "He's disabled and needs to rest a lot, so try not to make a lot of noise."

"Okay."

I watched out the window. We drove deeper into the mountains and the old car sputtered as it climbed the steep hills. Almost every turn was a hairpin. We'd drive straight for a moment, and just when it seemed like we were going to plow into the side of the mountain, the Buick would turn. I was glad I hadn't eaten, since I was beginning to feel carsick.

There was almost no flat land, so any houses either sat right near the road, or perched on the side of the mountain. They clung there, like dingy moths sitting on velvet drapes, and I half expected them to take flight at any second.

Finally, Samantha Rose pulled onto a dirt road with several driveways leading off it. A green street sign read CONLEY HOLLOW.

"This is us. Our house is just at the top of this hill," Samantha Rose said.

We passed a row of tilted mailboxes on rusty posts and I caught the name *Miller* written on the side of one before Samantha Rose gunned it. We drove by two trailers—a double-wide with a metal swing set, and a tiny one on wheels. An empty lot separated them from a small clapboard house that looked like it hadn't been painted in a hundred years. She turned the curve and suddenly we were in front of a nightmare.

"Welcome to the Hillbilly Horror Show," Hoyt muttered.

"Hoyt!" Samantha said. "What'd I say about keeping your pie-hole shut?"

But Hoyt was right; it was a horror. I stared out the window. The first thing I noticed was the trash. Soda bottles, scraps of paper, and waterlogged books littered the yard. A recliner with the stuffing coming out of it sat in a tangle of weeds next to some old cars and a rusty barrel.

Those were the highlights.

The house itself looked old as the devil and about as inviting. The front porch was crooked and crammed full of junk, too. I couldn't imagine living in that place. I'd rather sleep outside with one of the mangy dogs that were running around.

"Where are all the flowers?"

Samantha Rose put the car in park and turned to look over the seat. "What?"

"Mama said my grandma was good with plants."

"Oh." She shrugged. "There's a bush or two still around, but most of the beds have been taken over by weeds. Never had much use for gardening myself."

A thin, curly-haired boy who looked about my age came from inside the house.

"She's here!" he yelled over his shoulder. Two smaller boys raced outside, sending the screen door banging. They stared slack jawed as Samantha Rose parked the car.

"Who's that?" I asked.

"Neighborhood no-accounts." Samantha Rose opened the

door and stood beside the car. "What have I told y'all about coming inside my house when I ain't home?"

"Sorry!" the older boy called. I didn't think he sounded sorry at all.

Samantha Rose leaned down and looked inside the car at me. "You're gonna have to get out sooner or later."

I was too stunned by the state of the house to move. "Suit yourself," Samantha Rose said. She kicked a spotted mutt out of her path. "Hoyt, take the stuff inside and find a place for it."

I watched as Hoyt went around the rear of the car and pulled a box out of the trunk. SHRED was written on the side in Mama's handwriting.

"You getting out?" The sorry-not-sorry boy stood next to my window.

I nodded and opened the door. Castle Fields Mobile Home Park hadn't been anything to write home about, but at least it was neat. Our landlord, Mr. Randolph, would have had a stroke if he'd seen this place.

My new neighbor was shorter than me, and skinny, and his Dollywood sweatpants pooled around his ankles like clown pants. He smelled like sweat and tar.

"What's your name?" he asked.

"Wavie."

"That's a weird name. I'm Gilbert F. Miller. You coming to live here?"

"Maybe."

"Hey!" Samantha Rose yelled. For a second I thought she was yelling at me, but she was shouting at the kids still standing on the porch. "FRANK AND BEANS! Git!"

They both stuck out their tongues and jumped over the railing. I watched as they ran toward the old house across the field.

"If those two woke your uncle, I'll have their hides." She stormed up the steps and went inside.

"What's wrong with them?" I asked Gilbert.

"They're backwards." He moved closer and leaned against the car. "Their mama likes it that way though because she gets extra money from the government since they can't read. What about you?"

"What about me?" I asked.

"Can you read?"

"Yes. And write, too!" I blurted. Apparently you couldn't take those kinds of things for granted in Conley Hollow.

A loud rumbling began to grow closer. It sounded like the mountain was going to come down on us. "What's that?"

"Coal train. C'mon out back." He pulled my arm and dragged me around the house, past the piles of trash, to the end of the yard.

Gilbert pointed into the woods. "See the tracks?" he yelled.

The rumbling became a full roar and a train broke through the trees. The ground shook as the hopper cars, piled high with coal, passed. Gilbert picked up a small rock at his feet and hurled it through the air.

I heard a faint bang as it connected. "Won't you get in trouble?"

"Nah," he said. "I do it all the time."

After the final coal car was gone, it grew quiet again. I kept my back to the house and looked at the view, imagining Mama living here as a girl. The mountains sprang straight up beyond the train tracks, so tall I had to lean my head all the way back to see where they met the sky. The bright green leaves of the trees rubbed against each other in the wind, and the occasional bird flew from one tree to another, but otherwise it was quiet. I got the feeling that if I walked through the underbrush I'd be the first person since time began to touch the bark of those trees. Without the trash and the run-down house in view, it was so pretty it almost hurt.

The wind shifted and I smelled the faint odor of smoke. "Do you smell something burning?"

He lifted his arm and sniffed. "That's probably me. Gran needed help." He handed me a rock. "See how far you get."

I threw it toward the tracks and it disappeared in the brush. "Help with what?"

"Burning tires. You get the rubber off, there's metal underneath." He cocked his head sideways. "You moving here 'cause your mama died?"

I felt the same familiar kick in the gut. "Yes. How'd you hear?"

He hitched up his sweatpants. "People talk."

I couldn't argue with that. They talked at Castle Fields, too.

"You ever been here before?" Gilbert asked.

"Nope."

He pointed to the run-down clapboard house I'd seen earlier. "Well, over there's where Frank and Beans live. Their real names are Frank and Baily, but nobody calls them that. They live with their mama. Don't ask about their daddy. That's a sensitive subject."

We walked back to the front yard and Gilbert continued. "The fancy double-wide at the bottom of the hill belongs to the Rodriguezes. They're pretty new around here. They opened a restaurant in downtown Farley that's packed every Saturday night. They got a daughter about our age named Camille. Can't stand her."

"Why's that?"

Gilbert made a face. "'Cause she's a big know-it-all."

"How far away is Farley?" I asked.

He pointed. "A couple of miles that way, but there's not much to it. Want to know where I live?"

I shrugged.

"Right there in that trailer next to Camille's."

Since Samantha Rose's house was at the top of the hill, I could see the entire neighborhood. "What's across the river?"

"Woods, miles and miles of woods. I go exploring, if you ever want to tag along. I won't get you lost."

"Maybe." A thin path veered off from the driveway and headed into the woods. "Where's that go?"

"Angel Davis's house. It's back a ways, but when it's cold you can see the smoke from his chimney. He's old and crazy."

"Really?"

"Yeah, you'll see him walking around the Holler talking to

himself plain as day. Gran says he used to be a bigwig lawyer, till he got in trouble and lost his wife, his house, everything. Now he lives in an old shack and eats lost pets."

"Yeah, right."

"It's true," he said. "That's why all those stray dogs hang around. They're looking for their mates. Howwooooo!" He howled.

Hoyt came outside and jumped off the porch. "Mama wants you inside," he yelled at me.

He slapped Gilbert on the back of the head as he walked past us. "Quit messing with our water hose or you're gonna get it. I'm serious, Smelbert."

We watched as Hoyt walked down the dirt road.

"You figure out why she did it?" Gilbert asked.

I was confused. "What?"

"Why Samantha Rose took you in."

"Because we're related?"

Gilbert shook his head. "Nah. Samantha Rose ain't in the habit of doing anything 'less it helps her."

My heart sank. "She's that bad?"

He nodded. "As mean as they come. I'd sooner hug a prickly pear cactus."

"Great. And I'm stranded here."

"Don't let it bother you none. We look out for each other in the Holler. You're one of us now, even if your aunt ain't."

CHAPTER FIVE

Back in Andro, a woman at the Baptist church named Mrs. Parsons had two little foster children in her home. They'd come in and sit shoulder to shoulder on the pew and look real happy. Mrs. Parsons gave them coloring books so they wouldn't be bored. I was always jealous about those coloring books because Pastor Green's sermons were bottom-numbing boring with a capital OMG.

Once Mama offered Mrs. Parsons some of the clothes I'd out-grown, and we drove over to her home to deliver them. We stood in the living room of her tidy cottage while the kids went through the bags and thanked us. Mrs. Parsons moved away before I be-came an official ward of the state, but when things fell through with Hannah, and Mrs. Chipman mentioned foster care, I figured I'd land somewhere similar.

I was way off.

You entered Samantha Rose's house through the kitchen where dirty pots and pans spilled off the countertop onto the floor. A table made from plywood rested on sawhorses, and the remains of some meal—eggs or macaroni and cheese maybe—had hardened onto it. The bottom half of the window over the sink was broken and someone had covered it in cardboard.

Besides being filthy and cold, the house smelled like rotten eggs.

I'd never been under the impression that Mama and I were rich—you don't qualify for free lunches at school or get a food card from the fine folks at the Kentucky Cabinet for Health and Family Services unless you have financial difficulties—but this house was a whole new level of despair.

"Don't just stand there with your mouth open," Samantha Rose said. "Follow me."

I held my breath and concentrated on Samantha Rose's broad back as I followed her down a dim hallway.

"That there is your uncle Philson." Samantha Rose gestured toward a room on the right. "Best to leave him alone."

I caught a glimpse of a thin, bald man lying in a recliner with a newspaper spread across his chest. He looked at me without speaking, then yawned and closed his eyes.

"Your room is down at the end and Hoyt's is up in the attic. I wouldn't go up there if I was you."

I nodded. So far I hadn't seen a part of the house that I *would* want to go to.

Samantha Rose continued with her tour. "We only got one bathroom, so don't hog it. If you can't wash it in five minutes you ain't trying hard enough."

I cleared my throat. "I brought a toothbrush but we were out of toothpaste."

"Look under the sink." She stopped in the middle of the hallway and put her hands on her hips. "I only go to the store once a month and when we're out, we're out, so there's no need to ask."

"Yes, ma'am." I adjusted my backpack and it knocked against a frame hanging on the wall. As I reached out to straighten it, my heart skipped a beat. "Oh my gosh! This is Mama, isn't it?" I studied the school picture. "How old is she in this?"

Samantha Rose frowned. "Second grade, I think."

The hallway was lined with faded photos. I turned in circles, trying to take them all in at once. I stopped to study one that showed two girls in Christmas dresses. The younger girl was tiny, around two years old, with dark hair. Standing behind her was a blond girl of around seven. I recognized the frown. "This is you and Mama? You look so different."

"Everybody says that," she huffed. "Ronelda always was jealous of my long blond hair."

I used my fingers to wipe a path through the dust. "I liked Mom's hair—it came back even curlier after the last round of chemo." I took another step and stopped in front of a picture of two men sitting on a porch. "Is this this house?"

Samantha Rose sighed. "Yeah. That's Daddy on the left."

I peered closer. "So that's my grandpa."

She shook her head. "Dang! Don't know what I was thinking. Your grandpa is the one on the right."

"Oh. Who's the other guy, then? A brother?"

"Just a friend. Now how 'bout you save your questions till the conclusion of the tour?" She walked to the end of the hall. "Here." She pushed open a door. "This is your room."

I dreaded crossing the threshold, but compared to the rest of the house, it wasn't bad. A twin bed stood against a wall that looked like it was made from an old billboard. Someone had painted it white but I could still make out the faint words: *Marlow's Auto Parts*. A wooden desk and chair were tucked underneath a window. The room was full of old newspapers and piles of clothes, but there was no rotting food, and I could see a path to the window.

"This was Ro's side. Daddy put in that wall to divide it into two rooms years ago, so it's not big enough to swing a cat around in, but that there was Ronelda's bed."

There were several black trash bags of clothes on the bedspread, but I moved them aside and ran my hand along the wooden headboard. It was scratched and dusty, but it had belonged to my mother. I wouldn't have traded it for a golden feather bed.

"You can settle in. Later, I'll show you how to work the washing machine. There's a line out back, so you'll want to check the weather before you do your laundry."

When I'd first walked into the house, it had crossed my mind to call Mrs. Chipman and ask about my other living options. But now it didn't really matter. Nowhere was going to seem like home, and at least here I'd be surrounded by Mama's pictures and things.

"Thank you." I stared at Samantha Rose. "For giving me a place to stay, I mean."

Samantha Rose grunted once and closed the door behind her.

I THREW THE trash bags on the floor. Tomorrow I'd clean, but for now I dumped the contents of my backpack onto the bed. There was no closet, but the drawers of the desk were empty and would hold what little clothes I'd brought. I put my school yearbook on the floor near my bed and set the peony on the desk in front of the window. It needed light, so I pulled back the curtain. My room was on the front of the house, giving me a good view of the weeds and trash. I counted three lanky dogs, two spotted and one brown, snoozing.

Last year my class had studied President Johnson's War on Poverty. If the war was over, my new neighborhood was proof we'd lost.

Find a good life, Mama had said.

I looked out the window, imagining her as a girl wishing for the very same thing. Was she happy here? I had to guess not, since Conley Hollow hadn't been mentioned once in all my eleven years.

"What did you dream about, Mama?" I whispered against the glass.

My breath frosted the window and I drew a small heart in the moisture. I only had one dream, that Mama was still alive.

CHAPTER SIX

I spent my first weekend with Samantha Rose feeling like I'd ridden a Tilt-A-Whirl for too long—dizzy and sick to my stomach. With the loss of Mama and the shock of a new family, I figured the teeter-tottering sensation was normal.

I tried to balance myself by learning the 411 on life in Conley Hollow.

The coal train would roust me from bed, but I didn't mind. I wanted to be the first one up and out the door. With a five-minute limit on the bathroom, I didn't want to take a chance on anyone walking in while I was toweling off.

Hoyt was easy to figure. He'd smacked Gilbert on the back of the head and called him a name, so I liked him about as much as a toothache. He only had one gear and it was *s* for *stomp*. He stomped up to his room, stomped back and forth overhead and stomped back down for meals. He glared at everybody, me most of all. Even when I tried my sunniest fake smile on him, he just glared so hard I thought his eyes would fall out and roll off the table.

Uncle Philson was still an unknown. The only time he moved out of his recliner was to drag himself to dinner in his walker. And even then he didn't talk much, mostly sticking to one-word comments, like "Vinegar!" and "Milk!"

And Samantha Rose reminded me of rock candy, sugary sweet and hard enough to crack a molar. She threw around a lot of *honeys* and *darlin's* but they were always added on top of something bad.

"The toilet is clogged. How about trying your hand with a plunger, honey?"

"You'll be getting free meals at the school, so it'd help if you left the cereal for your uncle, darlin'."

"Detergent is expensive, so stuff as much laundry in as you can, honey," she told me. She pointed to the piles of clothes at our feet in the laundry shed. "Be careful picking it up. Mice like to hide in there."

Oh, okay. Also, gag.

I killed time by hanging out in my room (after I cleaned it, adding to the mountain of trash already in the backyard).

I was quickly filling my notebook with words that could be made from SAMANTHA ROSE. I knew there had to be hundreds and hundreds of them.

I'd written TRASH, TORN, TEARS, RAN, MET, RANTS, MONSTER on my first night.

Now I added HAMSTER, HORNET, MARATHON, SMOTHER, SNORE as I spied on my neighborhood through the window. I watched Frank and Beans playing tag, and Gilbert head off into the woods carrying a shovel and humming an off-tune country song, and the Farley Methodist Church bus come and go.

By Sunday afternoon my brain hurt from trying not to think, and I was ready to take a walk outside. I hadn't decided if I was staying, so there was no need to plant Mama's peony yet, but I wanted to look around for a good place just in case.

There was no sign of my grandmother's peonies anywhere, but the bushes Samantha Rose had mentioned turned out to be roses, with wild thorny stalks sprouting in every direction. I decided I would try to prune them later if I could find a thick pair of gloves. A bed by the steps held black-eyed Susans and lamb's ears, but they'd been nearly choked out by weeds. I was debating whether to start clearing it out when Gilbert turned the corner holding a pair of rusty binoculars. He was wearing the same Dollywood sweatpants and both knees were now grass stained. "Hey. See what I found?"

"Binoculars? Where'd you get them?"

"Found them exploring in the woods." He grinned. "You want to go spy on Angel Davis?"

"I thought you said he ate pets."

"Well, we ain't dogs, are we?"

I looked toward the path, hesitant. I was still figuring out life with Samantha Rose. She hadn't said anything about where I could go. I wasn't a hundred percent sure that she'd notice if I jumped on the coal train and never came back, but I didn't want to get in trouble.

A stomp sounded from inside the house signaling Hoyt was

on his way downstairs. So far today I'd managed to avoid His Surliness and I wanted to keep it that way.

"Okay," I said. I followed Gilbert out of the yard and toward the path. Wildflowers grew in lacy white clumps and I picked a handful as we walked.

"How far is it?" I asked.

"Just past the cemetery."

I stopped. "What?"

Gilbert jumped up and smacked a low-hanging limb. "Don't worry. It's not that big, just Holler people. And it's faster if we cut through it. You'll see Conleys make up a lot of the cemetery," Gilbert continued. "But there are others. Everybody in the Holler is connected in some way, even if it ain't blood." He turned to look at me. "Your mom's not buried there, right?"

"No, she's buried in Andro, where I used to live." I started walking. "She was cremated. Do you think that counts as buried?"

"Was she in the ground?"

"Her ashes were. In a biodegradable urn."

"If she was in the ground, I'd say it counts," Gilbert said. "What'd she die of?"

"Cancer." The word sounded just like the disease, hard and ugly.

"That stinks," Gilbert said. He picked up a stick and swung it back and forth like a baseball bat, smacking briars. "Almost there."

A few minutes later the path widened and we came to the cemetery.

"You too scared to go in?" Gilbert asked.

"No," I said. It was true. Once you've had the worst happen, there isn't much else to bother about.

Two redbud trees bloomed at the entrance. Their festive purple flowers announcing spring was here looked out of place against the scraggly ruins of the cemetery.

I pushed the gate open, and we passed a small concrete bench almost completely covered with weeds.

Gilbert pointed to two headstones and said, "Those say Conley," like I couldn't read.

"Hap and Louella Conley," I said. "My grandparents." I read the dates. "They died within a couple of years of each other. Samantha Rose said the last time my mom came back here was for my grand-mother's funeral." I did the math. "I would have been two."

"Since you're not afraid, you want to come up here some night and camp out? We could do a séance!"

"Not for a million dollars," I said.

Gilbert laughed. "For a million dollars I'd swim in Angel Davis's outhouse!"

"Gross!"

I walked around the other tombstones. "These say Conley, too. Check it out—this is for a kid. Darlene Conley, January 15, 1977, to April 17, 1979. Oh, how sad. She was just two years old." I bent down and pulled a couple of weeds from the front of the tombstone. There was something familiar about the story, tick-ling my brain just out of reach.

Gilbert looked around. "That one over there belongs to Alma Savage."

"Is that a relative, too?"

"No. She lived in the house where Frank and Beans are now. Gran said she got hit crossing the street in Lexington. Her husband went nuts. Took off into the woods one day and never came back." He held up the binoculars. "These are probably his."

"Really?"

"Oh, yeah," Gilbert said. "Who else would leave a perfectly good pair of binoculars laying around? Doesn't make sense unless you're"—he drew a finger across his throat—"D-E-A-D."

"Perfectly good? They're rusty."

"Well, they wouldn't have been when he left them. It's been over thirty years since he disappeared!"

I looked at the gravestone. "Alma Savage, 1948 to 1980. She was only thirty-two when she died. Are there any happy stories in Conley Hollow?"

He bit his lip, thinking. "Nope."

I pointed to a headstone in the corner that looked more cared for than the others. "Whose is that?"

"Angel's son, Delmore."

I walked over and looked closer. Weeds grew around all the headstones except this one. Someone had left a vase of flowers on top, and I pulled the dead blooms out of it, replacing them with the wildflowers I'd picked. I liked to think that someone in Andro was keeping an eye on Mama's plaque.

"He was young, too! What happened?"

"I forget. Gran would know." Gilbert headed toward the iron fence and hopped over. "If you want to see Angel's place we better hurry. It's going to be dark soon."

I climbed over and stood beside him. "Just for a minute."

We walked the path in single file, and just when I was about to say never mind, Gilbert stopped and handed me the binoculars. "Look through those trees over there."

The binoculars' lenses were caked with dirt. I pulled a leaf off the closest tree and wiped them. With three shirts to your name, you don't use them as napkins. I looked through the eyepiece. "I think I see a porch," I whispered. "And a rain barrel."

Gilbert nodded. "He sits outside a lot. Look for a cane chair on the left side."

I swerved the lens to the left and played with the mud-caked dial. A very thin, very old man came into focus. "He looks huge."

"Almost seven foot tall," Gilbert said. "I tried to send a picture of him to the paper saying he was Bigfoot but they wouldn't print it. Too skinny."

"Is Bigfoot supposed to be fat?"

"I guess the editors of the *Farley Gazette* think so. What's he doing now?"

I put the binoculars back to my face. "I don't see him anymore." I searched right to left. Suddenly he came into view, much closer to us, and staring straight at me!

I threw the binoculars to Gilbert. "He's walking this way," I said in a harsh whisper.

"Let me see," Gilbert whispered. He brought the binoculars up to his eyes and back down again. "Run!"

He didn't have to say it twice. I took off and didn't stop until I had jumped the fence, passed through the cemetery and was back on the road leading to Samantha Rose's house. Gilbert skidded to a stop beside me, gasping for air.

"For somebody who's not afraid, you sure run fast."

I grinned, then realized what I was doing and quit. Mama was barely gone and here I was moving on. Ugh. I had to be the worst daughter ever.

I picked another handful of flowers from the side of the road. "I better go inside."

"You starting school tomorrow?" Gilbert asked.

"Yeah."

"We wait on the bus down by the mailboxes. Be there early."

"Why?"

"You're the new kid and I met you first. I want to show you off!"

CHAPTER SEVEN

S paghetti noodles and ketchup, again. I tried not to groan. Mama hadn't made a lot of money working at Walmart, but she'd always managed to see that we ate well. My mouth watered thinking about her meat loaf. We'd even had lasagna on special occasions.

"Napkin!" Uncle Philson yelled.

Samantha Rose tore a paper towel off the roll and passed it over. "Would you look at these pretty flowers on the table? Wavie's only been here a couple of days and she's already trying to improve us." She twirled her fork in the noodles. "Conley Holler must seem like a step down from that fancy trailer park you're used to."

I shook my head. "I just thought they were pretty," I said softly.

"Pretty weeds," Hoyt said, chewing. He had a blob of ketchup on his chin.

"There's a school bus runs by here about seven fifteen a.m., and if you miss it you'll have to walk, sugar," Samantha Rose said. "Hoyt will show you where to stand."

"Yes, ma'am."

Hoyt made a face. "I don't ride the bus, remember? Zane picks me up on his way to the mine." He scowled in my general direction. "Just go down the hill until you hit pavement. If you get hit by a car, you've gone too far."

Samantha Rose snorted. "Hoyt, be nice." She took a sip from her cup and smacked her lips. "Wavie's got the right idea, make this place nicer. When y'all get home from school tomorrow, you can start helping with the cleaning. Wavie can take the kitchen."

I looked at the mess falling off the counter and onto the floor. The only way to make it look nicer would be to set it on fire and start from scratch.

Samantha Rose pointed her fork at Hoyt. "You can begin by picking up the trash outside. Right after school tomorrow."

Hoyt slammed his cup on the table. "Why do we have to get things all gussied up just 'cause she's here? Besides, I've got baseball practice!"

"Oh, Lord. God forbid you miss that!" She leaned back in her chair and rested her hands on her belly. "If talent was ink, you boys wouldn't have enough to dot an *i*. You're all sorry, every last one of you."

"We ain't that bad."

"Son, typhoid ain't that bad compared to your team. Give it up." Uncle Philson snickered.

I glanced at Hoyt. His face was cloudy with a chance of hail.

He glared at me. "Tell her to quit staring with those big cow eyes!" He jutted his chin forward. "Moo! Moo! See how you like it."

"Stop your fussing," Samantha Rose said. "Worry about your own self."

Hoyt stood up with a rush and knocked his chair backward. "I'm going out!" He stomped through the kitchen, slamming the door behind.

"Cheese!" Uncle Philson shouted.

I LAY IN my room thinking about Mama. Even on her old bed, with a blanket that still smelled like her lotion, the *not* of her was overwhelming.

A couple of years ago, when Walmart first came to town, she took me to the grand opening. They were giving away prizes to the first one hundred customers, things like a twelve-pack of Coke, and coupons for a free block of cheese. It was fun, but the most exciting thing was when the wind picked up and this huge balloon reading ANDRO WALMART broke loose. Everybody stepped out of line to watch it hang there, knocked back and forth by the winds. That's how I felt now. Like everything I was tied to was long gone and there was nothing to keep me from being blown into the side of a mountain.

I couldn't believe Mama hadn't told me anything about Conley Hollow. I thought of the graves I'd seen earlier. Did my grandmother even get to see me? I closed my eyes thinking back to everything I'd ever heard Mama say about her family. The small tombstone! The memory came back in a rush.

One of Mama's coworkers, Brad, had called to ask her for a date and I'd teased her about it for months. *Are you sure you don't want to go?* I'd asked. *I can spend the night with Hannah.*

We were snuggled on the couch watching reruns. *Nope. I wouldn't give up a night with you for anything.* She tucked the afghan around my lap, suddenly somber. *Do you miss having a man around the house?*

I don't know, I told her. *I can't really miss something I never had, right? But every now and then I think about what it would be like to have a brother or sister.*

She sighed. *Well, there's not much chance of that. But good friends can be like family.*

Did you have any siblings? I asked.

No, she said. *Mama had a baby girl, but she died young, before I was born. I don't think she ever got over it.* Mama's face turned sad like it always did when anything of the past came up, and we went back to watching the movie.

Samantha Rose had said she and Mama had a "falling-out." It must have been huge for Mama to lie her out of existence.

I heard the door open and sat up. Hoyt stomped in and stood at the end of my bed. His hair fell across one eye and he looked like a greasy redneck pirate. I pulled Mama's blanket up around my shoulders.

"You think you're all that, huh?" he asked.

"No."

"I can tell. I ain't stupid. You don't believe all that bull Mama said about wanting to take care of her dead sister's child, do you? What a joke."

I thought of what Gilbert had said. "Why'd she take me in, then?"

Hoyt smiled. One of his front teeth was crooked and overlapped the other. It gleamed a bluish white in the dark room. "Money, ya dummy. We'll be getting your Social Security checks soon. You're worth hundreds of dollars every month."

He laughed. "Wavie. It even sounds like the name of a cow."

"I'll tell Mrs. Chipman," I said.

"Won't do any good. The state don't care as long as they've got a place to put you."

I'd had about all I could take from my new cousin. "Hoyt?" I whispered. "Why don't you go play tag with the train?"

"Moo, moo, little brown cow." Hoyt stomped out of the room, still laughing. "You're a cash cow. Maybe we'll buy you a bell to wear around your neck."

CHAPTER EIGHT

There's a trick to crawling inside a window without sounding like a herd of elephants. Gilbert hadn't mastered it. On Monday morning he fell headfirst onto my bedroom floor.

Obviously, the concept of privacy hadn't made it to Conley Hollow. "What are you doing?"

He had his hand over his eyes. "Are you decent?"

"Yes," I whispered. "But get out of here before Samantha Rose finds you."

He waved a hand in the air like he was shooing away a fly. "Aw, she snores as loud as that coal train. Takes a lot to wake her. I need a favor. Here." He handed me a plastic jug.

"What's this?"

"Gran was a little short this month and the water got turned off again. Fill that up so I can wash off."

"You want me to fill this up so you can take a bath?"

"Yeah. Hoyt took the hose inside so I couldn't use it, but Mr. Vic won't let me ride the bus if I stink."

The last thing I wanted was to be caught with Gilbert in my bedroom, but I had to admit that he did kind of smell. Okay, he a lot smelled.

"Can't you go over to Frank and Beans's house?"

"Gran won't let me run up their water bill."

"All right," I said.

Gilbert grinned big and wide. "If there's any soap, throw that in, too."

The running faucet sounded like a waterfall but I made it back to the bedroom with the jug and a tiny sliver of soap without seeing anybody.

"I owe you one."

"Just go before I get caught," I whispered.

Gilbert climbed back out the window and reached for the jug. "I'll see you down at the road and you can tell me how to repay you."

"You don't have to," I said, but he was already off and running barefoot down the dirt drive.

THE DOG I called Spotted One met me at the bottom of the porch steps. I stood still to let him get a good whiff of my hand. "Are you going to bite me, or are we going to be friends?" I whispered. He nudged my hand with his cold nose and wagged his tail. "Friends, it is. Sorry. I don't have anything for you," I said, rubbing his head. "I'll have to find where Samantha Rose keeps the dog food."

Gilbert was all cleaned up, beaming bright as a police car spotlight. "Hey, Wavie. Meet Convict Holler's finest."

"*Convict Holler?*" I asked.

One of the boys, Frank or Beans, studied me with his mouth gaping open. "Don't you know where you live?"

"Nobody around here calls it Conley Hollow but the postman," Gilbert said, "and he's just obligated by law to say it correctly."

"You're ridiculous, Gilbert." This came from a girl with dark hair and dark eyes standing on the edge of the group. "Not to mention, your hair needs combing."

"Why do people always say 'not to mention,' then say it anyway?" Gilbert asked. "I'm trying to introduce Wavie to everybody. Not to mention, Camille, you're kind of hateful."

Camille stared at me, serious. "I heard your mama died."

I nodded. "Yes, six days ago."

"That's sad." She shook her head. "I'm sorry."

"Thanks." I set my worn backpack down at my feet. It was light. Samantha Rose hadn't given me any paper, but I had my notepad. It rested in the bottom with the picture of my mom. I considered taking the photo out and showing it to Camille, but there was a part of me that wanted to keep Mama all to myself. Besides, carrying around a picture of your mom was probably lame.

I rubbed my arms. Spring was coming slowly to Kentucky but the mornings were still chilly. My winter coat had been too small and too worn to bother packing.

"What grade are you in?" Camille asked.

"Sixth," I said.

"Me too."

"Camille's supposed to be in fifth grade with me," Gilbert said, "but she's *gifted and talented*. If you don't believe me, just ask her."

Camille smirked. "If you didn't skip school so much you'd be in sixth grade, too. Maybe not in the GT program, but out of fifth."

"Well, excuse me, Your Majesty," Gilbert said. "You ever thought that I don't want to be in any Gawky and Troubled classes?"

"If that's what GT stood for, you'd be sitting in the front row wearing a President of GT pin."

Gilbert ignored her. "We eat lunch at the same time, so you'll get to see me plenty."

"Good," I said, and I meant it. I'd been dreading the awkward lunchroom ritual of having to find someone to sit with and thinking of things to talk about. With Gilbert I didn't imagine I'd have too many quiet moments to fill.

The bus came around the curve and pulled to a stop in front of the group. The driver—Mr. Vic, I assumed—opened the door. "All aboard!"

I followed Gilbert, and Camille fell in behind us.

The bus was hushed. Sleepy bobbleheads on scrawny necks craned to get a look at me.

"Sit here," Gilbert said. He plunked down next to the window. "Have you thought about it?"

"What?"

"You know. What I can do to pay you back!"

I shook my head. "Not yet."

Camille sat in front of us and turned around. Her hair, a dark shiny waterfall, splashed on her shoulders.

I tucked a strand of mine behind my ear. I couldn't remember the last time I'd washed my hair: two, maybe three days at least.

"Why do you need to pay her back?" she asked.

"None of your beeswax," Gilbert said.

"You might as well tell me. The chances of you being able to help her on your own are slim and nada."

Gilbert made a face. "I knew as soon as I heard she was a girl you'd stick your nose in."

Camille looked down her nose at me. "Do you want to be his friend or mine?"

I thought of Hannah and the rest of the kids I'd known from the trailer park, now miles away in Andro. Without Mama, I was now ALONE, LONE, ONE. "Both?"

Gilbert groaned. "And I knew you were gonna say that."

"Make him pay you back," Camille said. "And make it hard. Otherwise he'll keep asking you to do stuff."

Gilbert turned to look at me. "As long as it doesn't involve broccoli. I hate broccoli."

"Why in the world would it involve broccoli?" Camille asked.

"I just wanted to get that off the table," Gilbert said. "It's what we call nonnegoatable."

"Non*negotiable*," Camille corrected.

"Isn't that what I just said?"

I leaned back against the seat and listened to the kids laughing and talking across the seats. My stomach unknotted a little bit with the thought of having two new friends.

THE PRINCIPAL STOOD greeting students with a handshake or a high five as they came through the door.

"Time for a lice check," Gilbert whispered. "That's Principal Rivers. She's a hundred years old and got more eyes than a two-headed spider. You can't get by with anything."

Camille rolled her eyes. "You're such an exaggerator, Gilbert! She's not a day over sixty and she's nice. Unless you do *something bad* like skip school to burn tires."

I was about to find out for myself. Principal Rivers motioned me over.

"Wavie, right? Let's go to the office and get you situated." She walked me down the hallway toward her office. A few minutes later, she slid a printed piece of paper across her desk.

"Your classes are listed here, and there's a map of the school on the back." Principal Rivers tapped the desk with the edge of her glasses. "Do you need to see the school counselor?"

"No, ma'am."

"All right. But know she's here if you need to speak to someone." She put her elbows on the desk and clasped her hands. "I knew your mama, you know."

I sat up straighter. "You did? When she went to school here?"

"That's right. You remind me of her." The principal gathered her papers. "If you're half the student she was, you'll do fine."

Personally, I thought schools put too much stock in grades, but that was probably because I hadn't made the honor roll in a while. Since Mama was smart, I always figured I took after my dad, He-Who-Shall-Never-Be-Mentioned.

"I'll try," I said.

Mrs. Rivers opened the door for me. "Great. And the most important thing is to come to class. If you have a problem at home preventing you from getting here, let me know."

I nodded and brushed past her. Gilbert was right. I could swear she was checking my head for lice as I went by.

"YOU WANT TO go exploring after school?" Gilbert asked.

Camille stared at him from across the table. "Who'd want to walk through briars and poison ivy to dig in the dirt, Gilbert?"

Gilbert slurped his milk. "Lots of people that aren't you."

"Did you have any problems finding your classes?" Camille asked.

"Not so far," I said. "The school's a lot smaller than my last one." I frowned. "I did get called on a bunch though. Half of my classes were empty."

"Mondays are bad," Camille said. "But it picks up as the week goes on."

"By Friday it'll be packed," Gilbert said. "That's when the fine ladies of Farley Methodist Church bring food for the impover-ished children." He clasped his hands together and pretended to cry. "Thank you so much for the Dollar General peanut butter, but could you please get creamy next time?"

Camille laughed. "I'll take yours if you don't want it."

"No way. A kid traded me four mac-and-cheese boxes for it last time."

"Did Samantha Rose sign you up for the Share-A-Lot pro-gram?" Camille asked. "You leave your backpack at the office on Fridays and they fill it up with food so you won't be hungry over the weekend."

"Yes," I said. "We had it in Andro, too, only the kids called it Shame-A-Lot. Everyone knew why you were going to the office on Friday afternoons."

"Well, you don't have to be embarrassed here," Gilbert said. "The whole school's on it."

"Nobody needs to be embarrassed, period," Camille said. "It's not our fault."

I picked up my fork. "She signed me up for free breakfast and lunches, too."

"Samantha Rose doesn't miss a trick," Gilbert said. "She sure knows the system!"

I thought about what Hoyt had said. "Boy, does she."

"What do you mean?" Camille asked.

I hesitated, considering how much to tell them. "How long have you guys lived in Convict Holler?"

"I moved in with Gran in second grade," Gilbert said. "I lived in the same school district before, so it wasn't a big deal."

I knew better than to ask him why he'd moved in with his grandmother. If you see a kid living away from both his parents, you can bet the history isn't good.

"We moved here last year from Texas," Camille said, "and it's been just awesome." She stabbed her chicken nugget hard.

"Gilbert said your daddy owns a restaurant?"

She nodded. "La Parrilla. That means The Grill. You can come with me sometime to eat, if you want."

"I'm in!" Gilbert said. He tilted his head sideways. "You meant free, right?"

"Yes, Gilbert, for free." She smoothed down her hair. "What's it like living with Samantha Rose? We can hear her yelling at Hoyt all the way down at my house."

"I'm still figuring it out."

"If she starts in on you, come to my house anytime," Camille told me. "My mom's not afraid of her."

"Gran neither," Gilbert said. "I don't know what it was like where you come from, but around Convict Holler we watch out for each other."

I looked around the lunchroom, making up my mind. Nobody was paying attention to us, but I whispered to be sure. "Hoyt told me last night that Samantha Rose only took me in to get my money."

"What money?" Camille asked.

"She's applied to be my guardian. That means she gets my Social Security checks. Hoyt said it was hundreds of dollars a month."

Gilbert whistled.

"You should tell somebody," Camille said. "It's not right for her to steal all your money."

"What's right got to do with Samantha Rose?" Gilbert asked.

I knew I should be mad, but I couldn't quite work up the steam. "I have a caseworker, but she'd probably say I haven't given it a fair chance, and maybe Samantha Rose will only take out my expenses."

Gilbert rubbed at a stain on his T-shirt. "Oh, the thing you can count on is her going through your money like a hog through corn. Samantha Rose ain't likely to get any better with time," he said. "But you're her family, so maybe she'll surprise us."

My experience with family was limited to Mama, but Samantha Rose was *nothing* like her. I hoped Gilbert was right, but I couldn't stop thinking of the notebook resting in my backpack. Yesterday I'd added more SAMANTHA ROSE words—TREASON, SHAME, SEAR and HARASS.

It felt like a bad omen.

CHAPTER NINE

Frank and Beans jumped off the bus in front of me and raced toward their house. I said goodbye to Gilbert and walked slowly up the dirt road, naming the wildflowers I could pick out among the greenery. Phlox, field mustard, wild ginger. No wonder Mama had loved flowers. She'd been surrounded by them growing up.

Samantha Rose was sitting outside on the front stoop smoking a cigarette with the box marked SHRED sitting at her feet. She took a last puff and threw the butt into the yard. "You get along all right at school?"

"Yes."

She pointed next to her. "Have a seat."

The step was only slightly wider than Samantha Rose, so I ended up with one leg slung over into the weeds.

She leaned down into the box and pulled out a piece of plastic. "I found this in your mama's things." She tossed it into my lap.

"Her checkbook?"

"Yeah. She have anything left? Or a savings account?"

"She closed it all right before she died." My voice cracked on that last word.

"Figures." She looked at me with narrowed eyes. "She give you any money?"

"No. There wasn't any to give once we'd paid the rent and the funeral home."

She snorted. "I guess Ronelda wasn't living so high on the hog after all."

I bit my lip. I wanted to tell her that at least our fridge was always full with real food. "Is that it? I've got homework."

Her head dipped once for yes. "Don't forget about the kitchen. And take that box out back. Hoyt can take it to the dump with the other garbage."

The kitchen was an epic disaster. It took me a full two hours to wash the dirty dishes piled on the counter, and by the time I'd stuffed them into cabinets, and stacked the pans under the sink, my arms felt like Silly String. The whole job was a waste of effort though, since it made about as much difference as spraying perfume on an outhouse.

I spread Mama's blanket on my bed and sat down crisscross applesauce. The homework portion of my conversation with Samantha Rose had been a lie. I'd finished it all in my last class before the bell rang. Hanging out at the hospital with nothing to do had put me way ahead in my schoolwork.

The checkbook dug into my back from where I'd stuffed it

into my pocket. I opened it up and looked at the figures. Just seeing Mama's handwriting made my breath catch.

I turned to the last page. The final entry was for twenty-three dollars and seventy-five cents to Walmart. Mama had been sick that morning but she'd insisted we go buy me a new pair of jeans. I'd said the pair I had was fine. Short, yes, but if I rolled them up they could pass for capris and who cared what Megan Harroway said anyway. But Mama wouldn't be persuaded otherwise.

I flipped through the check register. It was like a time machine. She'd paid rent on the first; before that there was a check to the Piggly Wiggly. There were deposits from her Walmart paycheck every two weeks until a month ago when she got too ill to go in at all. A few months before that, there was a payment to the Andro Credit Union for the car. The car was gone now, too.

I turned back another page. Thirty dollars went for my fifth-grade yearbook that I'd told her I didn't need, but she wouldn't listen.

"I never got one when I was a kid and it was the worst, Wavie. Don't tell me you want to sit there while everyone else gets all those squirrelly signatures. I know better."

Of course she'd been right.

I flipped another page and found a deposit for one hundred dollars. The entry read *Bowman*. I tapped the checkbook against my knee, thinking. The name didn't ring a bell. I looked at the date. The deposit had been made a week before my birthday. Mama had taken me to the pizza place next to the mall. Afterward we'd seen a movie, and not the cheap kind that comes out months after everyone has already seen it, but a brand-new one. I'd wondered how we could afford it, but I wasn't going to ask, not when a deep dish supreme was on the line.

Another page turn, another entry with the same *Bowman* written beside it, one hundred dollars at Christmas, then nothing for the year until my birthday again. There was another entry for the previous Christmas, at the beginning of the checkbook. Someone named Bowman had been sending my mom one hundred dollars for the last two years, maybe more, on my birthday and Christmas.

I uncrossed my legs and stood up. The tingling running up my backside could have been from standing suddenly, but I didn't think so. Mama had said that there was no family, yet here I stood. I hated thinking it, but I had to face facts. If Mama had lied about Samantha Rose, maybe she'd lied about other things, too. Like maybe my dad hadn't died before I was born, and maybe his name was Bowman.

Mama gone, a new aunt and a live dad? Since Mama had died, I'd been spinning faster than a merry-go-round pony. No wonder I was dizzy.

CHAPTER TEN

I didn't ask Mama about my dad very often because it made her too sad. One of the last times I did, I remember her telling me, *Jud? He was one of the good ones. His family was the worst, but he was cut from a different cloth.*

Is there a family resemblance?

You have his smile, she said. *And he was funny and optimistic, like you.*

So all I really knew about my father was that he'd supposedly died in a tragic accident before I was born.

Hope had burned me blacker than Mrs. Florence's biscuits before, but the words *what if* kept floating through my brain. *What if* he was alive? *What if* he wanted to see me? *What if* he didn't?

I put the checkbook in my back pocket. Looking for my dad would give me something to do besides watching the dogs chase one another around the yard. I didn't have to contact him, but it wouldn't hurt to have the option. Samantha Rose was in the living room fussing with Hoyt. If she saw me, there was no telling what disgusting chore she'd have me do next. I opened my bedroom window and crawled out over the sill.

ZANE'S PICKUP, WITH Hoyt's arm hanging out the passenger-side window, was heading down the dirt road loaded with the trash from the backyard. I covered my face from the dust and cut through the empty lot until I was standing in front of Gilbert's trailer.

A wiry older woman with short gray hair opened the door. She smiled sweetly. "Yes?"

"Hi. I'm Wavie Conley from next door. Is Gilbert home?"

"How do, Wavie Conley. I'm his gran. Hang on a minute." She turned, slow as molasses, and yelled into the room. "*Gilbert!* You got a friend on the doorstep!"

A few minutes later, Gilbert appeared in the doorway eating a piece of bologna. "Hey, Wavie. You decide to go exploring in the woods with me?"

I shook my head. "No. I've figured out what I want. How I want you to pay me back."

"All right." He rolled up the bologna and stuck it in the side of his mouth like a cigar. "How?"

I took a deep breath. "I want you to help me find my daddy."

"I was thinking more along the lines of giving you my fries at lunch, but I guess that'll do." He pulled the door closed and came down the steps. "Gran pretends she can't hear, but she listens in on everybody."

He leaned against the trailer. "When did you see him last?"

"Never."

"Oh." Gilbert chewed his bologna, thinking. "You think he's somebody your mama ran around with back in Andro?"

I shrugged. "No. She said she parted ways with the family after I was born, so I think he must have been from around here."

"You don't want to ask Samantha Rose?" He shook his head, answering his own question. "Nah, you can't trust her. C'mon."

I followed him through the weeds. "Where we going?"

"As much as I hate to admit it, Camille was right. We're going to need her help for something this big."

"Because she's so smart."

"No. Because we'll need to look him up online. Nobody in the Holler has a computer, but Camille helps in the library at school. She'll have the passwords."

IF CAMILLE WAS surprised at finding us at her bedroom door, she didn't show it.

A little boy of around five had announced his name was Edgar and led us through the trailer. Her double-wide was way nicer than anything back in Castle Fields Mobile Home Park. It was opposite Samantha Rose's house in every way imaginable.

It was clean.

It was new.

It smelled delicious.

Gilbert sniffed the air. "Does your house always smell this good? I'm about to lick the wallpaper!"

"Always. Dad's the chef at the restaurant, but my mother is just as good and I'm learning."

I looked around Camille's room. Star Wars posters were hanging nicely on every wall. "You like those movies?"

"They're okay. I want to be an aerospace engineer when I get older." She motioned for me to sit on the bed. "Gilbert, you can sit on the floor."

"If you think that bothers me, think again," Gilbert said. "I don't want your girl cooties anyway." He sat on the carpet and put his back against the wall. "If I was able to use the computer at school, I wouldn't be here now. Wavie needs help finding her daddy."

"That's what you get for trying to watch fishing videos during Technology class," Camille said. "I'll do an Internet search tomorrow. Where'd you see him last?"

"Nowhere. I've never met him."

Camille didn't seem fazed by that news. "What do you know about him?"

I sighed. "Nothing, really."

"But you have a name, right?" Camille asked.

"Maybe. I think it's Jud Bowman."

"That's a start. What else did your mama tell you about him?"

"Not much. Mainly that he was dead."

"That's gonna make finding him a little tougher," Gilbert said.

Camille stared at me. "Why are you looking for a dead father?"

I explained about finding the checkbook, and how Mama had also told me there was no family. "If she didn't tell me the truth about Samantha Rose," I said, "maybe she didn't tell me the truth about my dad." Outing Mama as a possible liar didn't sit well with me, but I didn't see any way around it.

"Gran didn't live here when your mama did, but I can ask her if she knows of any Bowmans," Gilbert said.

"Can I be honest?" Camille asked.

"That's another one of those weird things people say," Gilbert said. "Who says *please lie*?"

Camille ignored him. "Wavie, your mother might have had a good reason to keep you away from him."

"Yeah. She didn't mention Samantha Rose, did she?" Gilbert said. "Don't take a rocket surgeon to see why."

"Rocket scientist," Camille corrected.

"Ain't that what I said?" Gilbert asked. "Anyway, there's another possibility. He really could be dead."

"Well, somebody has been sending me a hundred dollars on my birthday and Christmas," I said. "Can you imagine Samantha Rose doing that?"

"I can imagine Samantha Rose stomping on your cake and making you eat the candles," Gilbert said, "but not sending money." He crossed his arms and frowned. "If we find your daddy, that means you'll leave."

"You're thinking way too far ahead," I said. "I'm not a hundred percent sure I want to meet him."

"If your dad *is* alive and not some scary criminal," said Camille, "why hasn't he stepped in now that your mom is, uh, gone?"

"Maybe he doesn't know her mom died," Gilbert said.

"Maybe he's alive, maybe he doesn't know. There's an awful lot of maybes," Camille said.

They were making me so woozy from the back-and-forth it was a relief to see a woman I assumed was Mrs. Rodriguez standing in the doorway.

"You are Wavie, yes?"

"Yes, ma'am."

She gave me a thousand-watt smile. "Welcome. We needed more niñas, right, Camille?"

Gilbert huffed. "I know what niña means—girl."

Mrs. Rodriguez wiped her hands on her apron. "I did not mean to offend, Gilbert. Would some chorizo queso help?"

"I don't know what that is, but if it's what's smelling up your house, count me in!"

Camille nodded. "Gracias, Mamá. We'll be right there."

CHAPTER ELEVEN

"Why aren't you eating?" Samantha Rose asked. "Something wrong with your mac and cheese?"

"I had a snack at Camille's."

"Who?" Uncle Philson shouted.

"The Mexicans moved in Tom Fuller's place," Samantha Rose said.

"Oh."

"Wha'd you have?" Hoyt asked, smirking. "Beans and rice?"

I rubbed my foot back and forth against a piece of torn linoleum. "Chorizo queso, actually." I smirked back. "It was delicioso."

"Oooh," Hoyt said. "Aren't you highfalutin?"

Samantha Rose dabbed her napkin at a cheesy patch on her lip. "How y'all communicate with them speaking Spanish and whatnot?"

"They speak English. Geez," I said. "And Camille's one of the smartest kids in school."

"Well, excuse me," Samantha Rose said. "How am I supposed to know what they can and can't do?"

"Milk!" Uncle Philson yelled.

Hoyt passed the carton across the table. "Why they got to move here anyway?" he asked. "Zane says before long Mexicans will take away all our jobs."

"Ha! That dropout makes a scarecrow look like a genius," Samantha Rose said. "Besides, you ain't got a job to start with. They going to take away your sitting on the couch doing nothing all day?"

I pressed my lips together trying not to laugh. There was only one thing that was okay about Samantha Rose—Hoyt wasn't safe from her sharp tongue either.

"I reckon Zane has a say. He's working."

"Mr. Rodriguez doesn't need Zane's mining job," I said. "Gilbert says their restaurant is packed on the weekends."

"If Smelbert said it, then it must be true," Hoyt said.

"Why do you always pick on Gilbert?" I asked. "You don't smell like a field of lavender yourself."

"Enough! Do y'all ever stop flapping your gums?" Samantha Rose yelled. She looked at me. "I thought you were gonna clean the kitchen this afternoon, sugar."

"I did."

"Then why is there a pile of dishes on the countertop?"

I pointed to Hoyt. "He brought those out of his room before dinner."

Samantha Rose frowned. "Nobody likes a tattletale, Wavie. We don't rat out people in Conley Holler, especially not family." She emphasized the word *family*.

Hoyt grinned.

"Why're you grinning like a possum?" Samantha Rose asked. "Did you take the trash to the dump?"

"Most of it," Hoyt said. "Zane's truck ain't all that big."

"The dogs got into the bag that was left," I said. "Trash is all over out there."

"You know what's important in Conley Holler?" Samantha Rose turned to me. "Minding your own business, that's what."

Hoyt snorted. "Wavie's minding the dog's business."

Samantha Rose laughed, and even Uncle Philson grinned, revealing a piece of noodle between two teeth.

"You mind going out and picking it up, hon?" Samantha Rose asked. "It'll give you time to think."

I didn't bother to argue. Samantha Rose wouldn't care that I had the beginnings of a blister where my sneaker was too tight or that the temperature had dropped. Besides, she was right. While I worked I'd think about a lot of things. Like finding my dad and leaving Convict Holler forever.

FOR A COUPLE that didn't work or leave the house much, my aunt and uncle managed to generate a bunch of trash. I walked back and forth picking up paper plates and food wrappers. Spotted One and Spotted Two sniffed at my jeans as I walked.

"You two can just go back and crawl under a car," I said, shaking my finger. "It's your fault I'm out here."

Spotted Two licked my hand.

"Really?" I wiped the slobber off on my pants. "That's a pretty gross way to say you're sorry."

The ripped bag was still lying in the front yard like a dead animal with its guts strewn about. I kicked a can toward it. Maybe I'd stay out here all night and catch pneumonia. Or crawl under the rusted car between the dogs—at least they liked me—and sleep forever.

Mama had called me an optimist, but I wasn't crazy. I was wising up fast and getting used to the fact that Samantha Rose wasn't going to like me no matter how much cleaning or weeding I did.

I finished picking up the trash and threw the bag against the house, being careful to miss the flower beds. Now that I'd cleaned out the weeds, the flowers were trying to make a comeback. I knelt down and brushed my fingers across a leaf of the lamb's ear thinking of what Mama could have done with this place.

She'd worked in the nursery department at Walmart and was so good at bringing plants back to life, her manager took to calling her Daisy Do-Over.

My thumb wasn't as green as hers, but she would have been proud of what I'd done with the yard so far. I plucked the leaf and stood, rubbing its soft surface against my face. I was supposed to be thinking of finding my dad, but all I could think about was Mama—and how everything I saw and did now would always be something I couldn't share with her.

I looked toward Gilbert's and Camille's and tried my best to hog-tie the jealousy I was feeling. Gilbert's grandma had practically oozed kindness and Mrs. Rodriguez had been all smiles and hugs and good-smelling food. They all had each other and I didn't have anybody.

I was staring so hard toward Gilbert's and Camille's that at first I didn't notice Angel Davis on the edge of the woods. Angel looked like a human version of the walking stick insect. He was skin and bones and seemed even taller than he had on his porch. His hair fell in a gray tangled mess past his shoulders. If a family of birds didn't live in his beard they were wasting an opportunity.

Spotted Two lifted his head and sniffed. It only took him a second to see Angel and start barking like a bear had just walked into the yard.

Angel's neck pivoted on its axis and swung my way. He stared up the hill to where I stood, frozen. "Spring beauty," he yelled, then turned and shuffled on down the dirt road.

I held my breath until he passed the mailboxes and disappeared out of sight. I didn't know if Angel Davis was dangerous, but he wasn't completely crazy. Spring beauty had been one of Mama's favorite flowers, and the common name for the wildflower I'd left on his son's headstone.

CHAPTER TWELVE

I didn't know how Angel Davis knew the name spring beauty or how he'd figured out that I was the one who'd put the flowers on the headstone. I asked Gilbert at the bus stop the next morning, but he didn't have a clue either.

"Are you sure you heard right?"

I nodded. "It was just two words. Spring. Beauty."

Frank and Beans chased each other in circles around us. Gilbert grabbed one of them by the arm. "Frank. You ever talk to Angel Davis?"

"Not if'n I can help it!" He jerked loose and lunged at Beans.

Camille jumped out of the way. "Did you ask your grandmother if she knew of any Bowmans?"

"Yeah," Gilbert said. "Sorry, Wavie. No luck."

"I didn't figure it'd be that easy," I said. What was?

"Can you two meet me in the library during third period?" Camille asked. "Mrs. Winn always eats a snack in her office the second half hour."

"That's Math class," Gilbert said. "Mrs. Webster is strict about hall passes, but I'll tell her it's an emergency." He hitched up his jeans. "I can only use the poop excuse once or twice a year, so I hope we find something."

"Eww," Camille said. She pretended to throw up.

"I'll do my best," I said.

Mr. Vic skidded to a stop in the gravel and opened the door. The bus was fuller today. As soon as we got on, a longhaired loud-mouth kid named Punk Masters started singing from the back of the bus, "Frank and Beans, good for your heart!"

Frank yelled, "Don't call him that!" and raced toward Punk with Beans right behind him.

"Frank! Beans! Find a seat," Mr. Vic said.

"My name ain't Beans," Beans yelled back.

"Butter beans, pinto beans, lima beans," Punk chanted. "Green beans, baked beans, Frank 'n' Beans!"

"Boys!" Mr. Vic yelled. "Unless y'all want a visit with Mrs. Rivers this morning, get yourself seated and fast."

The boys sat, but they continued to argue loudly with Punk. Martha Poston, a fourth-grader, grabbed Camille to ask her a home-work question. The commotion of twenty schoolkids screaming back and forth buzzed through the bus like an out-of-control drone, but it barely registered. In a few short hours, I might find my dad.

A FEW SHORT hours later, we hadn't found squat. No person named Jud Bowman existed in Farley, or Andro, or anywhere in the entire state of Kentucky. There was one guy with the same name in Minneapolis, Minnesota, but he'd just graduated from high school.

"Maybe Bowman is somebody else," Gilbert said.

"That's all the checkbook said? No first name or anything?" Camille asked.

"Nope. Just Bowman."

"That might even be the first name," Camille said. "Do you have the bank statement?"

"What good would that do?" Gilbert asked.

"The deposits are listed at the bottom. There's usually a copy of the check."

"How do you know that?" I asked.

"My father lets me help him with the banking for extra math practice."

"Lets you?" Gilbert sniffed his underarm. "If you move away, Wavie, who's gonna give me jugs of water?"

Camille shook her head. "Not me. Don't even think of knocking at my window. My father would have you in the Convict Holler cemetery before sundown."

"Who said anything about moving?" I slumped in the chair. "If the bank statements were in the box, they're long gone now. Hoyt and Zane took it to the dump."

Gilbert chewed on the end of his pencil. "I guess you'll have to ask Samantha Rose. If it was somebody that your mom knew before she left Conley Holler, she'd know."

"Probably," I said. "But she has a way of making the best

things sound bad. She could say cherry cobbler and it'd sound like a cussword."

"Y'all made cherry cobbler?" Gilbert asked. "That's my favorite."

"No, but if you're ever in the mood for noodles and ketchup, come on over."

"Uh-oh," Gilbert said. "I got trouble."

"What?" Camille whispered. "Do you see Mrs. Winn coming back?"

Gilbert stood up. "No, but now I really do have to poop. And I've used my number-two time with y'all!" He moved his chair and raced out of the library.

Camille rolled her eyes. "He makes me seriously loca."

"He's hilarious," I said. "How can you not like him?"

"Before I moved here," Camille said, "guess who had the highest grade point average in the entire school?"

I shook my head. "No way. Gilbert?"

Camille picked up a book off the return cart. "It's true. The only reason I've got better grades than him is because I study all of the time."

"So he's not in the GT classes because he really doesn't want to be?"

"Yes!"

"That's kind of silly," I said. "But why does it make you crazy?"

"Because he doesn't understand how lucky he is! He has a chance to get ahead and he's throwing it away, acting ignorant when he's not." She shook her head in disgust. My father has a saying, '*La persona que pide poco no merece nada.'* It means, 'The person who asks for little deserves nothing.' Do you think moving from Texas to the middle of nowhere to start a restaurant was easy?"

"No."

"No! But my father knew he had talent, so we took a chance. Gilbert is asking too little of himself and he's going to get nothing. What a waste."

"Maybe he's afraid he won't do as well in the harder classes."

"And I'm not? Everybody is scared of something, but you can't let it stop you. And you know Frank and Beans? They're not backwards, no matter what Gilbert says. They just stopped learning when they figured out their mama gets more money if they can't."

"Gilbert said the same thing. I don't get it."

"An 'intellectual disability' is worth more. My dad says these hills are full of smart people, but they don't see a future, so they don't even try to get out."

"My mom did," I said softly. "Get out of Convict Holler, I mean."

The warning bell sounded, signaling class was about to change.

"She was smart. And you are, too," Camille said. "Ask Samantha Rose about your dad before it's too late and you're stuck here forever."

CHAPTER THIRTEEN

As much as I wanted to find out about my dad, I wasn't eager to ask Samantha Rose. I decided to bide my time by working on the Conley Holler cemetery instead. I couldn't shake the idea that if I took care of the graves here, someone would check in on Mama's back in Andro.

Gilbert was off in the woods looking for more treasure and Camille was working on an extra-credit project, but I didn't mind being alone. It gave me time to think about Mama, and my maybe-alive, maybe-dead dad, without worrying I'd start crying.

My plan was to start with the weeds around Louella Conley's grave so that I could plant some perennials. According to Samantha Rose, Hap was mean, but Mama had come back for my grandmother's funeral, so she must have loved her. I was through the gate and halfway to the gravestone before I noticed the man sitting on the cracked bench. Angel Davis.

I stopped mid-stride. He hadn't seen me yet and there was a chance I could hightail it out of there before he did. That would be the smart thing to do when meeting a hairy giant, but I couldn't. He had the same look on his face that I wore on mine. Grief.

My sneakers made a swooshing sound as I moved to the tombstone, but he didn't turn around to look. The weeds were almost waist high and I quietly began pulling them out in large clumps, dumping them on the ground beside me. It felt good to be doing something of my own choosing, not something Samantha Rose had told me to do, and before long, I forgot about Angel. I cleaned Louella's, and then skipped over Hap's to do my mama's sister's.

While I worked, I planned. I bet I could find pink dianthus for the little girl's grave, and yarrow for my grandmother's. And I could transplant the lamb's ear for ground cover. Frank and Beans's mother, Mrs. Barnes, had some pretty flowers growing around her house. She might trade me a cutting for some of my grandmother's roses.

An hour later, the sun went behind a cloud and the smell of rotten eggs mixed with raging BO filled the air. I turned around and Angel towered over me.

"Were you the one that done it?" His voice sounded like he'd gargled with gravel and the smell of him, so nasty my eyes watered, hit me in a wave.

It took me a second to figure out what he was talking about. "P-p-put the flowers on the grave?" I stuttered. "Yes, sir."

He clawed at his beard with his hand. His nails were long and crusty. "I can't pay you, so don't bother asking. The money's all gone."

"That's all right," I said. I'd told Gilbert that I wasn't afraid, but

I couldn't keep my voice from shaking. I glanced up at his face. He had turned and was looking at his son's grave with sad, watery eyes. All the fright drained right out of my body.

"I was happy to do it." The longing for Mama was so intense it felt like my whole body was squeezing in on itself. I closed my eyes. "I lost someone, too."

Angel didn't answer, but I felt him shift beside me, and I opened my eyes. He was still staring at his son's grave. A fat tear rolled down his face, leaving a trail in the dirt on his cheek and landing to glisten in his beard.

"Do you think they know," he whispered, "that we're still here? That we miss them?"

My grandmother's headstone blurred in front of me. I'd wondered the same thing. "I think they must. All of the love and sadness and *feeling*, it has to go somewhere, doesn't it? Surely they feel it, too."

He nodded once and slowly lumbered toward the gate.

I began gathering the weeds around me into a pile. My fingernails weren't as bad as Angel's, but a dark line of dirt was visible underneath. I inhaled sharply, a stabbing ache in my chest, as a vivid memory of Mama came to mind.

It's a trick my mother taught me, Mama had said before we went outside to plant flowers in front of our trailer. She ran a bar of soap under my nails one finger at a time. *The soap will keep the dirt out while we're potting, and then it washes right out when we're done.*

I bet you're the smartest person in all of Andro, I told her.

I remember Mama's blue eyes crinkled at the corners when she said to me, *I don't know about that, but I'm the luckiest. There may be people in town with a better garden, but there's not a soul alive with a better daughter.*

I'd caught my breath on that word, *alive.* The cancer diagnosis was always there, hovering around us, threatening everything. Mama had bent down, hugging me to her. *Wavie,* she'd whispered. *We can't let fear of what might happen steal our joy right now.*

I can't help it, I said, burying my head into her shoulder. *What if you die?*

She kissed my temple and whispered in my ear, *Then you'll go on for the two of us, because it's only the thought of you living that makes this bearable. Life is for the living and I want you to have a good one.*

I wiped the tears off my cheek. It was a long time before I could see well enough to leave.

CHAPTER FOURTEEN

"Tell me again why we're studying on a Friday?" Gilbert asked as we were working at Camille's kitchen table.

"Because I need the help," I said. I had decided that if I was going to have the two smartest students in the school as my best friends, I might as well use them. Plus, there was nowhere I liked being better than at Camille's.

"But it's too nice out to stare at a textbook," Gilbert grumbled.

Camille slammed her notebook shut. "For the first time ever, I actually agree, Gilbert."

Mrs. Rodriguez turned from the stove to smile at us. "I think this group could use some fresh air and good food. Why don't you gather the plates and tablecloth and take them to the table outside? Dinner will be done in about ten minutes."

"Dinner, here?" Gilbert stuffed his book into his backpack. "Now we're talking!"

"Picnic, picnic, picnic!" Edgar yelled, racing for the door.

While Gilbert and Camille set the table, I gathered a few

blossoms from the side of the driveway and placed them in a small glass of water.

"Wow, that looks great," Camille said. "I recognize the honeysuckle, but what are those other flowers called?"

"Phlox."

"You're really talented, Wavie. We should tell my dad and get you to make some arrangements for the parties at the restaurant."

"Maybe," I said, like it was no big deal, like I couldn't feel myself glowing like a sunflower at high noon.

Mrs. Rodriguez brought out a platter and set it on the table. "Mrs. Barnes and her boys are outside. Gilbert, why don't you ask them if they want to join us?"

"Sure," Gilbert said. He stood and climbed on top of the picnic table's bench. "*Hey Frank! Y'all want to eat with us?*"

"Gilbert!" Mrs. Rodriguez said. "I could have done that! I meant walk up there and ask politely."

"Oh," Gilbert said. "Be right back."

We watched as he ran up the hill and spoke with Mrs. Barnes. He came running back and plopped down. "She said she had pinto beans on the stove, but thank you for asking."

Camille shook her head. "Beans for Beans. Punk Masters would have a big laugh at that."

"Thank you, Gilbert." Mrs. Rodriguez sat and began serving us. "I hope you like enchilada Suiza."

Gilbert sniffed his plate. "Enchilada whata?"

"Enchilada *Suiza*," Camille said. "Pulled chicken and creamy tomatillo sauce in a flour tortilla baked with Mexican cheeses." She took a bite. "Mmm. Also known as heaven on a fork."

I agreed with Camille, it was delicious. "Poor Frank and—" I stopped, remembering how mad Beans had gotten at Punk. "What is his real name again?"

"Baily," Camille said.

"Well," I said, "I feel sorry they're missing this! I've had plenty of pintos and they aren't nearly this good."

Mrs. Rodriguez handed Edgar a napkin. "Mrs. Barnes seems sad."

"Gran and her are friends. She says Mrs. Barnes got dumped and don't have sense enough to know it," Gilbert said. "Her husband went off to get work and hasn't come back. They're even worse off than us—and that's saying something."

"We shouldn't gossip about our neighbors, Gilbert," Mrs. Rodriguez said.

Gilbert's eyes bulged. "Who else would we gossip about? Besides, we ain't got cable anymore. It's all Gran's got for entertainment."

Camille and I laughed. He had a point.

"Why don't we change the subject," Mrs. Rodriguez said. "Where were you going yesterday, Gilbert? I saw you disappear into the woods."

"Exploring," he said. "I asked Frank and Baily to go, but they're afraid they'll get poison ivy or something this time of year."

Camille looked at me and pointed her fork across the table. "That's because he had it all over his face last year!"

"What happened to not gossiping about your neighbors?" Gilbert asked.

"That's not gossip! It's the truth!" Camille said.

"How'd you get it?" I asked.

"It was Punk's fault. He challenged me to a tree-climbing contest, then gave me the one covered in the stuff."

"Well, I know what poison ivy looks like," I said. "How about I give you all a lesson." I took another tiny bite, trying to stretch the meal as long as possible.

"I sure know now what it looks like, but thanks, Wavie." Gilbert rubbed his stomach. "This is the best thing I ever et! If you can cook like this, Camille, you and Punk Masters are gonna be real happy one day."

Camille threw her napkin at Gilbert. It bounced off his shoulder back onto his plate.

"Hey!" he yelled. "You're messing up my enchilada."

"Mention me and Punk Masters again and I'll mess more than that."

"Camille," Mrs. Rodriguez said. "Gilbert is only teasing you."

I grinned. "Mama used to say boys teased the girls they liked."

The looks of horror on Gilbert's and Camille's faces sent the rest of us bursting into laughter.

CHAPTER FIFTEEN

By the time I walked into our yard, I was feeling the happiest I'd been since coming to Convict Holler. The weather was part of it—the air smelled sweet and it was the kind of day that made you believe anything was possible. I stood looking down the hill. Frank and Beans weren't outside anymore but the window on the side of the house glowed a faint yellow. I could imagine them sitting around the table with their bowls of food, probably kicking each other under the table.

Gilbert had taken a plate to his grandmother and I could see them outside in folding chairs watching the sunset like other people watch cable TV. The picnic table had been cleaned up, and Mrs. Rodriguez had made a big deal out of taking the flower arrangement I'd put together inside. "I'm going to set it in the middle of the kitchen table so we can enjoy it with breakfast!"

It felt a little bit like I belonged here. That maybe things weren't perfect, but surely something good was still around the bend for me.

Then I noticed all the cars and trucks parked haphazardly in front of the house.

Other than Zane, Hoyt's mouth-breathing best friend, we never had visitors. I slowly opened the door and crept down the hallway. The living room was packed with strangers and country music was blaring from the radio.

Samantha Rose sat on the love seat next to a worn-out woman who looked like she'd robbed the makeup counter at Sears and put everything on at once. In a chair next to them was a brunette wearing cutoff jean shorts and a skimpy tank top. Two men in Appalachian Mining jackets were having a heated argument about Dale Jr. while Uncle Philson leaned back in the recliner almost horizontal. He was staring at a brand-new big-screen TV.

Samantha Rose motioned for me to come into the room. "It's the girl of the hour." She lifted a red cup in a toast. "To Wavie!"

The shorts lady laughed, then put a hand over her mouth as if it would hide the fact she was missing teeth.

"I was just going to my room."

"While you're up," Samantha Rose said, "hand me those pretzels."

The coffee table was littered with small bowls of tortilla chips, pretzels and popcorn. I passed the pretzels over and snagged a chip.

"I saw that," Samantha Rose said. "Aw, go ahead, have a handful. You might as well since you bought them." She doubled over with laughter. "Oh, Lord, you should see the look on your face!"

"Drink!" Uncle Philson yelled.

Samantha Rose scooted forward and heaved herself upright. "Who else needs a refill?" She collected the empty cups and looked at me. "Come help me. I only got two hands."

I followed her back to the kitchen. "Where's Hoyt?"

She shrugged. "Out with no-brain Zane, where else? As long as they stay away from the law, I don't care." She poured herself a drink. "I swear, when you frown it's like Ronelda's come back from the dead to rain on my parade again." She smirked. "She wasn't always Saint Ronelda, you know."

I put on my best fake smile. "I bet. Did she have a lot of friends in Conley Holler?" I asked.

She lifted the cup to her lips. "I don't know, the usual amount I guess."

"Drink!" Uncle Philson yelled from the other room.

"I heard you the first time!" Samantha Rose answered. "Lord, he's getting more impatient every day." She pulled a bottle out of the fridge. "Ronelda didn't have time for too many people 'round here."

She mixed a drink and took a sip. "Mmm, that's good. Why you asking about Ro's friends?"

I looked down at my hands. "She got a get-well card from somebody right before she died," I lied. "I didn't recognize the name."

"Well, I doubt it was from anyone around here or in Farley. Nobody was crying when she left 'cept Mama, and she'd been gone for years by the time Ro died."

I tried again. "Weird. So she didn't have any friends around here named Bowman?"

Samantha Rose coughed, spewing liquid on the countertop. "Did you say Bowman?"

I nodded.

"Those aren't friends. That's for darn sure. You should have thrown that straight in the trash."

"Why?" I asked. "Who are they?"

"Your saintly mama didn't tell you?" She wiped Ale-8 off her chin and smirked. "That's them fancy folks adopted you."

CHAPTER SIXTEEN

Samantha Rose mentioned me being adopted like she was discussing whether it was going to rain later.

"What?" I asked.

She stared with glassy eyes. "Your mama was so proud she was gonna get you a better life with those fancy people, and all that bull hockey." She took another sip of her drink. "Lasted eight days. I about split my gut laughing when that all fell through, I'll tell you that."

Everything she said was muffled and sounded like it was coming from far away. The music and laugher swirled around me like a cyclone. I spun out of the kitchen, down the hallway, ricocheting back and forth off the walls as I made it to my bedroom.

I leaned my head against the window and stared into the dark. The moon gave off a tiny bit of light and I could see my face, pale and stricken in the reflection. I didn't care about the Social Security money, having no dad, the horrible house, none of it mattered. I just really needed Mama and my old life and I was never going to have it again.

I wrapped myself in Mama's blanket and rocked back and forth on my bed, chanting, "Please let this be a dream, please let this be a dream, please let this all be a dream," until long after I heard the party end.

THE ROOM WAS bathed in early-morning light. I lay under the blanket that still smelled like Mama's lotion.

My mom was gone.

My mom was not coming back.

My mom gave me away.

It wasn't just that Mama had tried to get rid of me, which was bad enough; it was also that she hadn't told me a thing about it. We had shared everything. Wavie and Mama against the world! But no, she'd been taking money from this Bowman person for years and hadn't thought to mention it. She did *not* tell me that I was almost adopted. She did *not* tell me that they were sending money. And now she was *not* around to tell me why. The *not* of Mama was forming into a dark, hard ball in my stomach, and I could feel it spreading, turning my limbs numb.

MY STOMACH GROWLED, and I lay there debating whether to move. I didn't want to see Samantha Rose's ugly pie face ever again, but I was starving and I'd left my backpack of food in the kitchen. If I didn't hide a few things in my room before Hoyt got to it, it'd all be gone.

I swung out of bed and listened. Everything was quiet. The

radio that played country music all day hadn't been turned on yet. I opened the door and tiptoed down the hallway.

The remains of the party were everywhere. Paper plates, empty bottles and red cups were scattered across the coffee table and the floor. The whole room smelled like an ashtray.

I walked to the kitchen and was so focused on getting my backpack that I was halfway across the room before I noticed my uncle sitting at the table. He was wearing a stained T-shirt and a milk mustache. Hunched over his bowl, he looked like an old, pale turtle.

"Cereal?" he whispered.

In all the time I'd been there, we hadn't exchanged two words, and these were the first I'd heard him speak that weren't at full volume. Apparently, he didn't have any interest in waking Samantha Rose either.

I was about to say *no thanks*, since I got enough of watching him chew at dinner, but then he said, "You look like your mama."

Mama. The hard ball in my stomach moved to my throat. Almost adopted? It couldn't be real. Maybe Samantha Rose was a no-good liar who just wanted to keep me away from my dad. I pulled out the metal folding chair and sat down.

"You knew her when she lived here?"

Uncle Philson wiped his mouth with the back of his hand. "Everybody knows everybody 'round here."

I poured a heaping mound of cereal into a bowl. Let Samantha Rose wake up and see that! Being brave was a whole lot easier with nothing to lose. "Did you know my daddy?"

His head bobbed up and down. "Yup."

I ate slowly. "Is he alive?"

His mouth stopped in mid-chew. "Jud? Nah. Long gone."

I slumped down in the chair. "Samantha Rose said I was almost adopted. I guess she was telling the truth."

He shrugged and went back to chewing. "That's the way I heard it, too."

My cereal bowl blurred. I cleared my place and got my backpack and went back to bed. My mom was dead and there'd be no dad to swoop in and take me from Convict Holler.

I only left my room once more on Saturday. I planted Mama's peony deep in the dark soil by the front steps.

I wasn't going anywhere.

CHAPTER SEVENTEEN

"**I** need orange juice, and toilet paper, and a scratch-off lottery ticket," Samantha Rose told me on Sunday morning. "If there's anybody in the store, Robby Billingsly will tell you that you're too young to buy one, so just nod and hand him the five. He'll bring it out by the ice machine when everybody leaves."

I didn't want to go to the store for Samantha Rose. I didn't want to get out of bed, period, but there was the matter of the lack of toilet paper to contend with, and Samantha Rose was not going to be the one to get it, thank you very much.

Camille had gone to church with her family, and Gilbert had boarded the Farley Methodist Church van. I'd been invited to attend by Gilbert via the bedroom window, but even the promise of cookies and cherry Kool-Aid couldn't tempt me to go.

Almost adopted. I would have never known my own mother. I felt like the trees were closing in on me, making it hard to breathe.

I limped down the highway. The blister on my heel rubbed against the back of my sneaker with every step. I loosened the laces and tried walking on the front of my foot as much as possible, but it didn't help.

Almost adopted—until my mom changed her mind. Or the Bowmans changed theirs. Almost someone else's daughter. My feet shuffled against the asphalt, putting rhythm to my thoughts. Al-most, al-most, al-most.

The Farley Get-N-Go was about a mile ahead on the right. I'd seen it on the morning drives to school, but I'd never been inside.

I heard the door ding as I walked in, and a large man sat perched on a thin bar stool behind the counter. He looked up briefly before going back to his *Truck Trader*.

I walked up and down the aisles, touching the brightly colored packages of chips and cookies. It seemed like a hundred years ago that I'd had a mom and a cookie jar full of my favorites.

Frank and Beans's mom was standing in the next aisle looking at medicine. I'd only seen glimpses of her standing outside when the boys got home from school. Up close she was nothing but sharp angles. Her elbows looked pointy enough to cut right through the sweater she wore, and her hands were thin, with long bony fingers. She set the medicine box down and picked up another, then traded them out again, before heading toward the counter.

"I thought you said he had a fever," the man behind the counter said to her. "This is for constipation!"

"Oh," Mrs. Barnes said in a small voice. "I must-a grabbed the wrong one."

"That would have been a messy mistake," he said, chuckling.

Mrs. Barnes turned pink and wrung her thin hands.

I set the orange juice and large package of toilet paper I had tucked under my armpit on the floor. "I'll get it." I walked back to the medicine aisle. Neither one of the two medicines that Mrs. Barnes had been debating over were for fever. It only took me a second to find the right one and take it to the counter.

"Thank you," Mrs. Barnes said as she gathered her coins and left.

I handed over the money for the items and the lottery ticket.

Standing on the tips of my toes, I watched her out the window as she walked, head down, back toward Convict Holler.

CAMILLE SET HER lunch tray down on the table. "In Kentucky, the birth mom, that's what they call it, birth mom, has ten days to change her mind before the adoption becomes final," she said. "I looked it up while Mrs. Winn was on her phone."

"I told you I don't care," I said.

Gilbert hunched over his food. "I bet that's why these Bowman folks were sending you money. They were trying to buy you back."

I crossed my arms and stared at the crumbs on my napkin. "I told y'all. It doesn't matter either way."

"Wavie," Camille said. "I didn't know your mom, but I think I get it. Didn't Samantha Rose say your mom was bragging about how awesome those folks were? Your mom must have wanted you to have a better life."

"I guess."

"I wonder what happened," Gilbert said.

"Isn't it obvious? I can barely let go of a really good library book," Camille said. "Imagine how it must have felt giving away her baby. Your mom must have changed her mind before the ten days were up. But there's a way to find out for sure."

I shook my head. "I am not asking Samantha Rose anything else. Ever."

Camille tucked a strand of hair behind her ear. "I wasn't talking about her. I think you should find the Bowmans."

"Yeah," Gilbert said. "Give 'em your new address. You might be getting two hundred dollars a year for the rest of your life!" He grinned. "I reckon that might be a lot of dollars by the time you turn eighteen."

Camille slammed her milk carton onto the table. "You know good and well, Gilbert F. Miller, that seven times two hundred is fourteen hundred. Stop pretending to be as dumb as you look."

Gilbert frowned. "Why should I?"

"So you can make something out of yourself and get out of Convict Holler?"

"Hey, how'd we get on me? I thought we were talking about Wavie."

"Well, now it's your turn. You are a big fat phony."

"Say what now?"

Camille pointed her straw at Gilbert's chest. "I know that you don't care a thing about basketball. You only tried out for the team last year because Punk Masters did."

"I do too like basketball," Gilbert said. "Everybody knows that."

"Really?" Camille smirked. "How'd the Wildcats do last season?"

Gilbert pulled at his shirt collar. "I don't remember. TV was out a lot back then."

"I bet. Why do you take a book when you go fishing? I've never seen you come back with anything but a sunburn."

"Charles Dickens isn't noisy," Gilbert said. "What should I do while I wait, play the trombone?"

"Would you two stop fighting?" I said. "You both have giant superbrains. You should both go to college. And maybe I can get a job at the mine."

"I'll be right there with you," Gilbert said. "Gran ain't got the money to pay for college." He stood up and picked up his tray. "And studying won't make a lick of difference." He marched off toward the trash cans.

"You have to admit he's right," I said. "Gilbert's got the brains and no money. Samantha Rose is taking my money, and even if she didn't, I don't have the brains. We're as stuck as day-old eggs on a cast-iron skillet."

"You do the dishes again this morning?" Camille asked.

I snorted. "Who else? Hoyt?"

"So you're saying there's no hope for people like us?" Camille asked.

"I'm saying if there's hope in the Holler, it's on an extended vacation! I know it, Gilbert knows it, even Frank and Beans know it." I grabbed my tray and stood up. "The only one who doesn't know it is you."

CHAPTER EIGHTEEN

I was afraid that Camille would be mad at me for yelling, but she'd acted sad more than anything else. In fact, the whole bus had seemed depressed that afternoon. There was the same old laughing at goofy jokes, and the singing of "Frank and Beans, good for the heart, the more you eat, the more you fart," but the closer I'd looked the less sincere it all seemed. Punk Masters grinned, but it was more feral than happy, and even Mr. Vic's hearty "Hello!" had sounded tired.

I'd watched Gilbert tease Martha Poston and they both had the same faded look about them that screamed, *We are poor*.

Maybe it was because we all had raggedy backpacks at our feet, empty now of donated food, reminding us that we were the have-nots. Even Camille, with her daddy and his restaurant, stood in line for the Shame-A-Lot food. Not one person on that bus had what Hannah and I had called Backpack Parents.

Hannah. It felt like years since we'd been in school together, whispering about the kids who had parents who bought them new backpacks every year and filled them with all the items on the school list, not just paper and pens.

I LOOKED AT my desk. The yearbook Mama had insisted on buying me was hiding under a pile of old homework, and I pulled it out. I set it on my lap and flipped through the pages. Marlena Spears had Backpack Parents; we'd watched her daddy carry her backpack into school on her first day like she was too pretty and delicate to handle it herself.

Christie Lee had Backpack Parents, too, and so did Melanie McDermid, and Katherine Shelby. I studied their pictures. There was something shiny about them all. You could tell just by looking at them that they didn't ever worry about how long they could make a pair of jeans or sneakers last. And they probably never ate spaghetti and ketchup for dinner.

My picture was on the right side of the page. There was nothing shiny about me for sure. My hair was parted straight down the middle and wet. I'd been up with Mama all night. She'd thrown up for hours, so I'd overslept and barely had time to get out of the shower and to the bus on time. It didn't look wet in the picture; it looked greasy. The photographer had told me to tuck my chin in, which only made me look like a Flat Stanley drawing.

I slammed the book shut and tossed it on the bed. The only thing shiny about me had been Mama. If she'd been so insistent for me to have a life, she shouldn't have left.

Camille wanted me to find the Bowmans. For what? I grabbed

a sheet of paper out of my notebook and a pen. A-D-O-P-T-E-D—DEAD, DOPE, TOAD, DAD. I crumbled up the paper and threw it on the floor. Even if I found them, what would I say?

The whole situation made me madder than a yellow jacket stuck on fly tape. Mama was gone, Samantha Rose was part demon, and now I was just supposed to write to these strangers?

I wanted to scream at Mama for giving me away, but she wasn't here. How'd they convince her to give me up anyway? I thought of Samantha Rose and the smug way she'd just blurted out the whole story. What I'd give to wipe that smile off her face. If I yelled at her, well, it didn't warrant thinking about. That left the Bowmans—the people who'd almost taken me away from my mama. "Why'd you keep sending money?" I whispered. "Did you feel sorry for us?"

I imagined them sitting in a fancy subdivision house, looking down their noses at us. I bet they could tell that even as a baby I wasn't like them. "Is that why you sent me back, because I wasn't good enough for you?" I put my pen against the clean sheet of paper and began to write in thick, angry strokes.

> *Dear Bowmans,*
>
> *You adopted me once, or so I've been told from a very unreliable source. If it's true, I'm writing to tell you something—I'm glad you gave me back to my mama 'cause she was the best person that ever lived! I don't care that we were poor, or that now I have to live in Convict Holler*

because she died, 'cause it means I got to be her daughter.
And I'm mad I even had to be apart from her for those
eight days!

   I don't know why you kept sending money, maybe you
felt guilty, but don't worry about it. I wouldn't have fit
in anyway because I'm not that smart or beautiful. And
I'd rather be an orphan like I am now than to never have
known my mama. So there!

                                        Not yours,
                                    Wavie Boncil Conley

The Buick drove into the yard and beeped. I tore the letter out
of my notebook and stuffed it in a drawer. It felt good getting all
my anger down on paper.

"Get out of the way, you old goat!" Samantha Rose yelled from
outside.

I pulled back the pink curtain and watched as Angel Davis
shuffled toward the driver's side.

"Philson, get him away from me!"

Uncle Philson slowly opened his door and hung on to the
frame. "Go on now, Angel."

Angel scratched at his beard with his long fingernails. "I told your
daddy I'd keep you girls together. You should have gone with
your sister!" He shuffled closer. "I should have said no to Hap!"

"Stop coming around here with your crazy talk. Get away
from me!" Samantha Rose yelled. She put a hand over her nose.

I smiled. I'd been up close to Angel. That smell would be with her for a long time, and I found myself wishing he'd touch her hair or her clothes with those fingernails. That would be the grossest thing ever.

But he didn't. He just yelled, "You girls were supposed to stay together" one more time, then walked out of the yard, leaving Samantha Rose's scowling face behind.

CHAPTER NINETEEN

My second Social Security check came and this time both Hoyt and Samantha Rose got cell phones. I barely even cared. The only thing I needed was a new pair of sneakers since I was beginning to get blisters on all my toes now. But I wouldn't ask Samantha Rose for shoes if the whole world turned to glass.

I'd just finished dressing for school when Gilbert knocked at my window. As usual, he had his hands over his eyes.

I pushed the window up. "It's okay, Gilbert. I'm dressed. Where's your jug?"

Gilbert dropped his hand and grinned. "Don't need it. It's the best morning out and I'm going to the river. Wanna come?"

The sun was shining and a warm breeze rustled the curtain. "You're skipping school?"

"It won't hurt this once." He hitched his jeans up onto his bony hips. "It's a great day to go find more treasure."

"Rusty binoculars aren't exactly treasure, but I'm in."

Gilbert grinned and gave me a thumbs-up. "Don't go to the

bus stop, Mr. Vic might see you. Meet me under the bridge." He moved away from the window. "Oh, and bring something to eat if you can. No free lunches today!"

THERE WEREN'T A lot of choices in Samantha Rose's kitchen, so I had to be careful. She'd notice if I took too much. I found a plastic bag and poured a cup of cereal into it. In the refrigerator there was an open package of hot dogs. I threw one, along with a piece of bread, a dill pickle and some saltines, into another grocery sack and put it into my backpack. I'd seen Gilbert eat, so it wouldn't last us long, but I was used to days with less.

Conley Hollow looked pretty in the morning sun. Trees, already thick with green leaves, jutted up on all sides, and the river, a thin, silver bracelet, glistened brightly at the bottom of the hill. Spotted Two wagged his tail from underneath a rusty car, too lazy to get up and follow me.

Gilbert peeked out from under the concrete bridge and waved me over.

"What are you doing with a fishing rod?" I asked.

"I had to tell Gran something." He hid it underneath the bridge. "C'mon."

I followed behind him, careful where I put my feet. The banks were covered with rocks, slick with water and algae.

"Where are we going?" I asked.

Gilbert picked up a stick and pretended to hit a baseball. "Through the woods to where I found the binoculars. They were stuck under a rock in the ravine, so they didn't get washed away. Maybe other stuff's stuck up there, too."

"How far from here?"

"A couple of miles or so. We can just follow the river," Gilbert said.

"So what are you talking about? What stuff?"

Gilbert put the end of the stick against the ground and leaned on it. "I'm talking about Marley Savage. I think those binoculars really did belong to him. Maybe we'll find his rifle or canteen or some old coins. That part of the river is still fairly wild, so hopefully no one else has beat us to it."

"Who's Marley Savage again?"

"The guy that took off years ago when his wife died. No one ever found him, remember?"

I had an uneasy feeling. "We're looking for old bones? What makes you think he died? Maybe he just left this place for somewhere better."

Gilbert shook his head and lowered his voice to a whisper. "Nah. He went into the woods upset about his wife's death and he never came out. Hunters say when the moon is full they can hear him up there crying for her." He grinned. "And when I solve the mystery, I'll finally get my name in the *Farley Gazette*."

"Why do you want to be in the newspaper so bad?"

Gilbert's mouth turned down at the corners. "'Cause." He dropped the stick and started walking. "We've still got a way to go."

"'Cause why?" I asked, following. "What's so special about the *Farley Gazette*?"

Gilbert didn't turn around, but he told me. "My mom is up-state in the federal penitentiary. Gran sends her the paper every week to keep up with what's happening around here." He wiped his face with his T-shirt. "I thought it'd be nice for her to read something about me. All right?"

I swallowed the lump that had suddenly formed in my throat. "All right. Let's keep moving."

We walked farther and farther from Convict Holler. As the river got narrower, the brush and briars grew thicker and Gilbert had to clear a path for us with his stick. It was peaceful except for the sound of birds, and trucks on the highway above.

It was a relief when we reached a wider, shallow portion and we could walk on the bank again. I found a large boulder and sat down, taking my shoes off and sinking my toes into the cool sand. I hadn't walked outside barefoot since last summer and my feet were as white and soft as marshmallows.

Gilbert stopped. "Why'd you take your shoes off?"

"I need to rest a minute. Besides, it's so beautiful here. If we couldn't hear the semis, I'd swear we'd gone back in time."

He squatted down in the sand. "Yeah. I bet if we had a picture of this spot from a hundred years ago, it'd look exactly the same."

I looked around at the old maple trees along the riverbank. The rock I was sitting on was the perfect place to rest. "I wonder if my mama ever came here. I bet she did, don't you?"

Gilbert nodded. "It's hard to resist a place like this near the water." He threw a leaf into the stream.

"Smooth it glides upon its travel,

Here a wimple, there a gleam—

O the clean gravel!

O the smooth stream!"

His voice was soft, but it echoed through the valley.

I stared. "What the heck was that?"

Gilbert's cheeks turned pink. "A poem. You ain't ever heard of Robert Louis Stevenson?"

"Yeah, but I don't know anybody that can recite him." I grinned. "You really *are* full of secrets, aren't you?"

"Whatever. C'mon. If we're where I think we are, the ravine should be just up ahead around the bend."

Gilbert huffed and puffed in front of me as we climbed.

"Hey, I found the ravine," Gilbert shouted.

I dropped my backpack at my feet. A deep gorge ran straight up the mountain. If it held the bones of Marley Savage, Gilbert would have a tough time finding them, because the mountain was covered with trash.

"What happened?" I asked. "It looks like a train wreck."

Gilbert flung himself down onto the ground. "Nah, just people too sorry to take their stuff to the dump."

"So they just throw it here? Down the mountain?"

"There must be a road up at the top. Which means it ain't the area where I found the binoculars. Darn."

"How'd we miss it? I thought we just needed to follow the river."

"Everything looks different from this perspective. Maybe we should have tried one of those side cricks."

I sat down beside him. "You want something to eat? I've got dry cereal and a hot dog and bread."

"I'll take the hot dog, I guess," he said glumly. "I know you probably don't think we're gonna find Marley Savage or his stuff."

He was right; I didn't. But just because hope didn't spend much time in Convict Holler didn't mean I wanted to squash what little of it there was.

"So you'll keep looking. You're bound to find him sooner or later. Who else is even thinking about old Marley Savage?"

"That's true." He wrapped the hot dog in the bread and took a big bite. "Still wasted a lot of time walking."

I looked up at the ravine full of trash. "Maybe not. You and Gran take stuff to the recycler, right? I bet we could find something up there—enough pop bottles for a six-pack of Ale-8 maybe."

Gilbert pulled his shoulders back and smiled. "That's good thinking, Wavie B. It'll make up for not bringing home any fish, too."

I emptied half the dry cereal into my mouth and handed the bag to Gilbert. Neither one of us had thought to bring a drink. We were so parched by the time we finished the saltines, we risked drinking water from the river.

"With my luck we'll get typhoid fever and die," Gilbert said. He looked over his shoulder. "Sorry, Wavie."

"Ugh." I wiped my tongue on my T-shirt. "Sorry that you killed me with nasty river water?"

"For mentioning dying. I never had a friend with a dead parent. Incarcerated, yes, but not dead. Am I not supposed to mention it?"

"It's okay, Gilbert," I said. "Sometimes I feel like I'm the only one that remembers Mama's gone. Samantha Rose hasn't said her name in weeks." I leaned down and picked up a smashed can. "Want this?"

"Takes too many," Gilbert said. "Bottles, wire, bigger chunks of metal is what we want."

I handed him a grocery bag and we moved slowly up the mountain, grabbing trees to hang on to as we climbed. Every few feet we'd stop and put stuff inside. When we reached the top, it was even worse than below. Someone had tacked a sign to a tree that read NO DUMPING, but it clearly hadn't stopped anybody.

"You got room in your bag for this?" Gilbert yelled. He held up a hubcap. "My bag is about to break."

"I'll stuff it in my backpack. It should fit."

Gilbert bent his elbow and aimed the hubcap like a Frisbee toward me. I jumped but it flew over my head and hit the ground, rolling, rolling, and finally coming to rest against a cardboard box. The sun filtered through the trees, reflecting off the hubcap, blinding me. I dropped my backpack and knelt down to unzip it. That's when I saw it. The box that had stopped the hubcap's progress had one word written on the side in handwriting I'd recognize anywhere. SHRED.

CHAPTER TWENTY

I pointed to the box with the familiar writing on it.

"What's wrong?" Gilbert asked.

"Hoyt and Zane. They were supposed to take the trash to the dump but they didn't!"

"Figures. Probably pocketed the ten-buck fee instead. So?"

"So, this is the box with Mama's papers." I bent over and peeled back the cardboard sides. It was full of envelopes. Some were marked *Hospital Bills*, or *Tax Receipts*, but the majority had the Bank of Andro logo on the upper left corner.

Gilbert dropped down beside me. "The bank statements! Which one do you need?"

I flicked a roly-poly bug out of the way. "Look for envelopes postmarked June or December," I said. "That's when the checks came."

We pawed through the papers. It hadn't rained recently, but they were stiff from where the sun had dried off the mornings' dew. Gilbert grabbed big handfuls and put them on the ground beside me. "I'll scoop, you look."

"March, September, February, bingo! Here's December." I pulled it out of the stack and held it against my chest. My heart was beating like I'd just run up the ravine. I frowned. I didn't even want to find these people, so why was I so excited?

I emptied the envelope onto the ground and picked up the statement. The printout listed all the checks by number and, at the bottom, the amounts credited to the account. Below each number was a scanned printout of the check. It was the second one, right under Mama's payroll check from Walmart. Two weeks before Christmas, Mama had received a hundred dollars from John and Anita Bowman. Their address was printed right under their name.

"They're from Lexington," Gilbert said. "City people!"

It wasn't their names, or the fact they were from a big city, or even that seeing the check made it real that was making my stomach do flips. It was the section on the check where it said *For*. In pretty, delicate handwriting, it read *Wavie*.

Samantha Rose would notice if I came home early, so Gilbert and I hid by the bridge until we saw the bus deposit Frank, Beans and Camille onto the side of the road. As soon as they went inside, I ran up the hill.

Samantha Rose was sitting at the kitchen table eating macaroni and cheese out of its microwavable container. "They give you any more of these at school?"

"No. But Gilbert has extra boxes. You want me to trade him something?"

"Trade? How about you tell him I won't call the law on his skinny tail for stealing my water the last two years." She pointed to a chair. "Have a seat."

I plopped into the uncomfortable metal seat. "What's up?"

"Mrs. Chipman called," Samantha Rose told me. "She wants to schedule a home visit."

At the mention of Mrs. Chipman's name, my heart skipped a beat. My favorite class at school was Technology, and I'd used my fifteen minutes on the computer last week to research guardianship. I had learned one important thing. There would be a *hearing where the minor child's best interests are taken into account.*

"When's she coming?" I couldn't keep the hope from rising just a little bit. Mrs. Chipman had promised Mama she'd find a good home for me. If anyone had my best interests at heart, it was her.

Samantha Rose's eyes narrowed. "You're not thinking of pulling a Ronelda and skipping out of Conley Holler, are you?" She laughed, a short, raspy bark. "Only Ro's kid would be dumb enough to dream about foster care. You are just like her, aren't you, hon?"

I gritted my teeth. I might be mad at Mama for giving me away when I was a baby, but she'd been funny and kind, and not dumb at all. "I hope so," I said.

"Fine, dream all you want. But if you say something to Mrs. Chipman to make it seem like you don't like it here, we might have a problem, sugar."

"She told Mama the final decision would be up to me." I'd

barely gotten the words out of my mouth when Samantha Rose smacked me across the face.

I couldn't have been more stunned if she'd pulled off a mask to reveal an alien head. No one had ever hit me, ever. It hurt like the devil. I put my hand on my cheek. It stung with the heat of a thousand fire ants. I'd never hated anyone before, but now I had a good idea what it felt like. My eyes filled with angry tears.

"Oh, don't look at me like that with those big doe eyes; I barely touched you. I'm just trying to wake you up to reality." She put her hand under my chin and lifted my face. "Your mama is gone and we're your family now."

"I have rights," I whispered. "It says so right there on the state website."

"I know this is hard, sugar," Samantha Rose said. "You're still young and think life is full of happy endings, but it ain't. . . . So let me tell you how this is gonna go. We're gonna meet with Mrs. Chipman and you're gonna tell her how happy you are here. You don't have any other family, and there ain't a foster home in this county that wants to go up against me. You understand?"

A tear ran down my face. It felt cool against my hot cheek. "Yes."

"Good." She stood up and stretched. "I'm glad we've got that settled. If I go to town later, you want to come?"

I shook my head.

Samantha Rose shrugged. "Suit yourself. I'm taking a nap." She lumbered out of the kitchen and down the hallway.

When I heard her bedroom door close, I picked up a spoon

from the table and held it so that I could see my reflection. My right cheek was beet red but other than the lone tear, I'd managed to keep from bawling. I wasn't sad anymore. I was E-N-R-A-G-E-D—ANGERED, DERANGE, GRENADE. I may have been poor, and possibly stupid, but when my mama was alive I was loved. She would have gone crazy on anyone who'd hit me. She once made a salesperson at Target cry because they said orange wasn't my color!

I shoved out of my chair and went to the sink. I ran a cloth under cold water and placed it on my cheek. I could see Convict Holler through the window. It wasn't a bad place; Mama and I could have been happy here. We could have been happy anywhere, but I wouldn't stay with Samantha Rose if she lived in the middle of Disney World. And as soon as my face stopped throbbing, I was going to make a plan and get as far away as possible.

CHAPTER TWENTY-ONE

At school the next day, Mrs. Rivers gave me the same high five, but this time it came with a side of disappointment. "I missed you and Gilbert yesterday."

"Influenza," Gilbert said. "It's a killer."

Mrs. Rivers crossed her arms. "I'm amazed that you've recovered so fast. Do I need to quarantine you two in detention to make sure it doesn't spread?"

"No, ma'am," I said. "It won't happen again." Conversing with the principal about skipping school was a new one for me, but I was too distracted by the bank statement in my notebook to give it the concern it would normally warrant.

Camille had an appointment this morning, so her dad was bringing her to school. I was dreading showing her the statement. I still didn't know how I felt about the Bowmans. One minute I was ready to dig out the hateful letter I'd written and mail it to them. The next I was remembering how happy Mama and I had been at the pizza parlor on my birthday. The hundred dollars they sent must have made Mama's Christmas a lot easier, so it was hard to despise them completely.

Since Camille was late for school, she had to take her lunch in the library and do a makeup test. By the time we finally saw her on the bus heading home, Gilbert was bobbing up and down like he was riding a pogo stick. "You've got to tell her before I bust!"

"Tell me what?" Camille asked. Her hair was pulled back in a shiny ponytail. In fact, everything about Camille looked shinier. She was even wearing a skirt and it looked expensive, like it had come from Sears or JCPenney.

I pulled the statement out of my notebook and handed it to her. "Gilbert and I found Mama's box. Stinkin' Hoyt and Zane dumped it on the side of the road."

Her eyes got big. "Wow. And it wasn't ruined?"

"Hasn't rained in forever," Gilbert said. "We got all kinds of good trash."

Camille read it quickly. "So here it is. You've got their address. Now what?"

"Now I'm considering my options."

"What do you mean?" Gilbert asked. "Before, you thought it might be your daddy." He slumped over the bus seat. "Finding him would have really been something. We could have called the *Farley Gazette*," he said. "They are always running photos of soldiers and their families reigniting."

"You mean reuniting," Camille said.

Gilbert shrugged. "Same thing."

Camille looked at me. "Are you going to get in touch with the Bowmans?"

"Yes. No. I don't know. What do you think?"

"What for?" Gilbert asked. "Because of the money? Even if they did keep sending you checks, Samantha Rose would just get it."

"Only if she found them." I turned to lean in closer to them and whispered, "I'm not staying here, not with Samantha Rose. Yesterday, she slapped me."

"Wait. What?" Gilbert said. "She slapped you? Live and in person?"

Camille rolled her eyes. "No, Gilbert, virtually." She grabbed my hand. "Are you okay?"

A hot rush of shame swept over me, but I said, "I'll live. It only stung a minute."

Gilbert punched the seat with his fist. "One of these days I'm gonna get off my leash and Samantha Rose will be my first dog biscuit."

"Down, boy," Camille said. "Why did she hit you?"

"She said she was trying to wake me up to the reality of my situation, but I'm going with she's the devil." I pushed my bangs out of my eyes and clipped them to the side with a rusty bobby pin I'd tucked in my pocket.

"Can you call Mrs. Chipman?" Camille asked.

"Samantha Rose would lie her way out of it, you know she would. If I only had a little bit of money." I stopped.

"Wavie," Camille said. "What are you planning?"

I crossed my arms. "Coal trains go by every single day. One of these times I might just hop on one and ride it to the end of the rail." I looked out the window. "Mama said to find a life. Anywhere is better than Convict Holler."

"Oh, there are worse places to be," Gilbert said. "Besides, running away always ends bad. Don't you watch those *detective* shows on television?"

"Well, I can't stay here," I said. "Every time I look at Samantha Rose or Hoyt, I want to scream."

Camille pressed her shoulders back against the seat. "You're right. But you're not going to write the Bowmans and ask for money."

"I wasn't going to just blurt it out. But if they offered . . ."

"No. Gilbert's right, asking for money and running away is a horrible idea. But contacting them isn't."

I had a sick feeling that I knew what Camille was going to say before I asked, but I asked it anyway. "If I'm not writing for money, why bother?"

She smiled. "To see if they want you back, of course."

A paper airplane soared overhead and Gilbert knocked it out of the way. "What can it hurt?"

"Seriously? You two are nuts!" I said. "I wish I had a cell phone just so I could text LOL to the both of you." I put my hand against the back of the seat and pretended to write. "Dear Anita, hey, remember me? You changed my diaper for eight days? Good news, I'm available again!" I threw my pretend pen down. "See. Y'all are insane."

"Now you're acting as silly as Gilbert," Camille said.

"Hey!" Gilbert said. "I resemble that!"

"Resent," Camille said.

"That too," said Gilbert.

I couldn't help but laugh. Gilbert and Camille might have crazy ideas, but at least they were on my side.

Punk Masters yelled from the back row, "Frank and Beans, gave me gas."

"*Shut up*, Punk, I can't hear!" Gilbert shouted.

"You shut up!" Punk yelled back.

"You two are forgetting one thing," I said. "What if it wasn't Mama's idea to stop the adoption? What if they decided parenting wasn't all it was cracked up to be?"

"You were a baby," Camille said. "Everybody loves babies."

"I don't," Gilbert said. "They're loud. God should have made a way to put them on vibrate."

"Most normal people love babies," Camille corrected. "Your mom probably got cold feet. Besides, why would they send you money if they didn't want anything to do with you?"

"Guilt?" I turned to look out the window. "I was their kid for eight days, so technically I've had two moms and two dads and lost them all. I'd be better off running away. At least I'd know what to expect."

Camille frowned. "Yes. A whole lot of trouble."

"Unlike the Disney sitcom life I've been living," I said. "Until I know for sure that it wasn't their idea, I'm not writing a word."

"Argh," Camille said. "We're going in circles! We need to get more information. What if we ask someone who was around back then?"

Gilbert rubbed his head. "What someone? Samantha Rose?"

"No, but maybe a friend, or the lawyer that handled the adoption," Camille said.

"Oh!" Gilbert said. "So all you have to do is find the person that handled Wavie's almost-adoption eleven years ago. Yeah, that's gonna happen."

I hugged my backpack. "You are going nuts."

Camille raised one eyebrow. "My mother always says, 'If you want the fruit you must climb the tree.'"

"Maybe I don't want the fruit," I said. "Maybe it's poisonous."

"Or maybe you'll get your hopes up and be disappointed?" Camille answered. "I get it."

Gilbert frowned. "I don't know what fruit trees have to do with anything, but y'all are making me hungry."

Mr. Vic pulled the bus off onto the road's shoulder and opened the door.

Camille grabbed her backpack and stood up. "If it was their idea to stop the adoption, then you can do whatever you want. Deal?"

I sighed, then reluctantly nodded. My mama had a saying, too. Beggars can't be choosers.

CHAPTER TWENTY-TWO

Finding out about the adoption and why it fell through would require help. Grown-up help.

Mrs. Rodriguez set a dish in front of Gilbert. "Try this. My husband claims my guacamole is the best in the world, even better than his."

Gilbert sniffed. "It's green."

"Yes, and the most delicious thing you'll ever put on a chip, I promise," Camille said.

I picked up a chip. "I'm ready if he's not."

Mrs. Rodriguez passed out napkins.

"Gracias," I said.

"De nada. Now, everyone, dig in," Mrs. Rodriguez said. She sat on the stool next to Camille and put her elbows on the table. "Tell me again about this lawyer?"

Camille explained as best she could.

"Almost adopted? And you want to know why?" Mrs. Rodriguez asked.

"I know it's crazy," Camille said. "But Wavie's afraid giving her back was their idea."

"I doubt that," she said. "But there's no one else to ask? A friend of your mom's maybe."

I shook my head.

"Edgar," Mrs. Rodriguez called into the living room. "Pick up your toys, please." She turned back to the table. "Well, Camille has a cousin in Texas that was adopted."

"Oh, yeah!" Camille said. "I forgot about Petra."

"A few years ago, Petra decided to try and find her birth family. She used one of those websites where adoptive children can look for their birth families, and vice versa."

I slathered a chip with more guacamole. She was right; the dip was awesome. "But I already know my birth family."

"Yes, but you could put in the town and the dates. Perhaps someone knows the names of lawyers around here that handled those types of cases."

"Wow," Gilbert said. "There ain't no slack in your rope, Mrs. Rodriguez. I'm impressed!"

Mrs. Rodriguez smiled. "I don't know what that means, but thank you, I think."

"I'll work on it tomorrow while I'm in the library." Camille stared at Gilbert. "And you don't need to come. No more number-two issues."

"Gilbert?" Mrs. Rodriguez said. "Are you all right? Do you need prunes?"

She looked confused when all three of us burst into laughter.

SAMANTHA ROSE KEPT me so busy cleaning the house over the next few days that I didn't have time to think about what would happen if Camille really did find the lawyer.

My favorite job was dusting the pictures in the hallway. I was still mad at Mama for leaving me with so many questions, but one look at that familiar face would send all ill feelings scattering. I wiped the photo of Samantha Rose and Mama in their Christmas dresses. "You're way cuter," I whispered to Mama. "And about a zillion times nicer."

I pulled down the photo of my grandpa on the porch and wiped the frame. Something fluttered from the back and landed on the floor. It was a newspaper article. I leaned down and picked it up. Underneath a grainy photo read:

MARLEY H. SAVAGE MISSING AND PRESUMED DEAD

The Farley County Sheriff's Department called a halt to the search for Marley Savage yesterday after a torrential rainstorm. "It's been three weeks," said Sergeant Grundy, "and any trace has been lost now to the weather."

Mr. Savage was reported missing on February 17 by his friend Hap Conley when he didn't return home from hunting. Mr. Conley said Mr. Savage had been despondent at the death of his wife, Alma Savage, several months before.

Searchers have combed the mountain for days, but no trace has been found.

A fund has been set up for the Savages' two daughters at Farley First Union.

I kept the newspaper article to show Gilbert, and rehung the photo. There were two men in the shot. One that Samantha Rose had said was my grandfather Hap Conley, so the other one had to be Marley Savage. He looked vaguely familiar, but it could have just been the sad look on his face. There were a lot of those around here. I looked at the other frames hanging on the wall. Several held the same man. He must have been a good friend of my grandfather's.

"What are you doing standing around?" Samantha Rose said. "You don't have enough to do?"

"I was just looking at this picture of my grandpa."

"Well, quit looking." She moved in front of the picture. "Go outside and knock back some weeds. It looks plumb snaky."

"You want me to garden?"

"Yeah, and today would be nice. And don't be jaw jacking outside with your friends. Your uncle Philson is trying to sleep."

I DIDN'T HAVE to worry about keeping my friends quiet. Camille was studying for a test, and Gilbert was out looking for Marley's bones. Even Frank and Beans were nowhere to be found. I was on my lonesome.

Samantha Rose had said to garden, but she hadn't said where, so I headed to the cemetery.

The iron gate squawked as I pushed it open. A blue jay complained loudly about it from a nearby tree.

"Sorry!"

I looked around. The grave sites of my grandmother and aunt were a little bit better from my earlier weeding, but Hap's and the rest, except for Delmore's, were still a tangled mess.

I'd brought an old pair of scissors, and I sat down to hack everything within reach. It was slow going, but after an hour, I'd cleared the tallest weeds from Hap's and Alma's graves. My hands were aching and there was a big blister on my thumb.

I lay out on the grass and stared up at the oak leaves. If Mama hadn't left Convict Holler, she'd be buried right here. And if I'd stayed with the Bowmans I'd have never met her. Loneliness and grief hit me like a steamroller, pressing me into the grass. I felt like I was about to sink underground and mingle with the bones of my grandparents.

Find a good life—Mama might as well have just told me to grow wings and fly to the moon. Maybe her list would have been different if she'd known I was headed for Convict Holler. *Stay in your room, be quiet, and when you can, go far away.*

I sat up. Something was different. A twig snapped on the other side of the clearing where the path disappeared into the woods.

I peered into the shadows. "Gilbert," I called, hoping.

Angel Davis stepped out from behind a tree. He shuffled forward and peered through his long gray strands of hair. "Spring beauty."

We hadn't talked since the last time we'd met in the cemetery but he didn't look any better. "That's right. It was one of my mama's favorites."

Angel came closer to the fence. He was so tall it barely hit his knee. "I thought you were dead."

I shook my head. "Nope, just lying here on the grass in front of a headstone."

His Adam's apple stuck out like he'd swallowed a small bird. It bobbed up and down as he spoke. "No one comes up here anymore but me and you. Nobody else remembers." His watery eyes looked straight through mine. "That's not right, is it?"

"No," I said softly. "Everybody ought to be remembered."

"You're not dead?"

I stood up and dusted off my jeans. "I feel like it sometimes, but no." I walked over to the gate and pushed it open. "You coming to visit your son's grave?"

He nodded.

The wind shifted and I caught a good whiff. He didn't smell any better than last time either. "I'm leaving now but if you want, I'll plant some flowers over there when I do the others."

The bird in his neck bobbed again. "That'd be all right."

I waved bye and left the cemetery. Angel was crazy and sad but I'd take that over mean any day.

Once I'd asked Mama what made people so mean.

It's the hardness of life you're seeing, Wavie. That's what makes people act that way.

But you're not hard, I'd said. *Life hasn't made you like that.*

That's because I fight it, honey. Sometimes it's like walking up a muddy hill in slippery shoes, but you have to keep trying. Once you let

yourself go down to the bottom, it's hard to ever recover. Don't ever stop
fighting.

That's what it felt like now, like I was sliding down that muddy hill fast, and Samantha Rose was waiting at the bottom.

I looked past Samantha Rose's tired, old house toward the highway. I'd never been far, but I knew the road led to homes with two-car garages and fenced-in yards and moms that were still alive.

Why did some people seem like they were born with mountain climbing shoes on and nothing but flat, green grass in front of them while I had two dead parents and a house full of hard-faced kin?

Edgar ran out of Camille's trailer and jumped onto the swing set. The Rodriguez family didn't have a whole lot more than the rest of us, but they seemed happy. I felt an ache deep down in my marrow so painful I had to catch my breath. I had been happy too, before.

Mama said life made people hard, but maybe she was wrong. Maybe it was moms that made the difference. My mom had kept the hardness away and now that she was gone, there was nothing to stop its coming.

CHAPTER TWENTY-THREE

Camille dropped her tray down on the table. "Okay. I have really good news. Also, some really bad news. Which do you want first?"

Gilbert rolled a carrot around with his fork. "Can we just have the one?"

"I wish." She bit her thumbnail. "I am seriously freaking out here."

"Tell us the good news!" I said. "Then we can decide if we want to hear any more."

"Okay." She placed both hands on the table and paused dramatically. "I think I found the lawyer who did your adoption!" She squealed. "Can you believe it?"

"You're joking," Gilbert said. "How?"

"It was on one of the adoption registry sites. I check it every day when I'm helping Mrs. Winn, and today I had a notice in the inbox!"

My heart stuttered. "Oh my gosh! What did it say?"

"It was from a woman named Josephine Logan. She's from the county next door and she's looking for her birth daughter."

"She told you all of that?" I asked.

"Oh yeah. She said to share it on Facebook—like I have an account! Anyway, turns out that she used an attorney from Farley. She said he handled adoptions for lots of people in the area."

"What's the bad news?" Gilbert asked. "Is he dead, too?"

"No," Camille said. "Not exactly."

"So he's only sort of dead. That seems about right," I said.

"He's not dead at all," Camille said. She took a deep breath. "I don't know how to say it, so I'm just going to spit it out. The attorney's name is Ralph P. Davis."

"Get out!" Gilbert said. "You're making that up."

"What's the big deal?" I asked. "Who's Ralph P. Davis?"

Camille frowned. "Nobody calls him that, Wavie. Around here he's known as Angel."

I dropped my fork. "The sad, stinky Angel that hovers around the cemetery like a grief-stricken giant?"

"Sí. The very one."

"Makes perfect sense to me," Gilbert said. "Everything and everybody in Convict Holler is connected somehow. Now we just need to ask him about the adoption."

"Sure," I said. "Did I mention that yesterday he thought I was dead? The man actually believed he was talking to a ghost."

"To be fair, you were in a cemetery," Camille said.

"And you are kinda pale," Gilbert added.

"So what do you two think I should do?" I asked. "Hang out over the graves until he comes back?"

"First thing we do is find out how crazy he really is," Gilbert said. "And I know just who to ask."

"**GRAN,**" **GILBERT SAID.** "We need your help."

The three of us were sitting elbow to elbow on one side of the table in Gilbert's tiny trailer.

It was the first time I had seen inside and I was surprised at how nice everything was. There wasn't much space, but everything was organized. A tiny refrigerator sat under a tiny stove. The kitchen was barely as big as the hallway in Samantha Rose's house.

"Where's your bed?" I whispered.

"You're on it," Gilbert said. "The table lowers down."

"Y'all want some cathead biscuits?" Mrs. Miller asked. "I made 'em this morning. They're cold, but they're good."

She didn't have to ask twice. Gran put the plate of big round biscuits between us with a jar of jam. "Help yourself. Those strawberries grew right on this mountain."

"Gran," Gilbert said, spreading jam. "What's the 411 on Angel Davis? Is he crazy or dangerous?"

Mrs. Miller sat down on the other side of the table and stirred a spoonful of sugar into her coffee. "What's a 411?"

"It means information," he said.

"Why didn't you say so?" she asked. "And why you asking about Angel Davis?"

"He lives right here, ain't that reason enough to wonder?" Gilbert said.

"How can he live up there like a hermit?" Camille asked. "Doesn't he have to leave for groceries? Or get his mail?"

Gran leaned her elbows on the table. "I don't reckon he needs much. He's got a well and a garden. I seen Bertha Loftis's pickup truck parked over by the pathway every now and then." She took a sip of coffee. "She helps him put up beans and taters ever year, so with that and the groceries she gets for him, he probably has enough to get through the winter."

"He's a lawyer, right?" Gilbert said. "What happened to that?"

Gran nodded and began to tell us the story.

"Angel Davis was born Ralph Patrick Davis. He was tall like his daddy, and so puny his shoulder blades stuck out like angel wings through his shirts—so that's how he got his nickname.

"By the time Angel started high school, he wasn't only the poorest kid in three counties, but also the tallest. The basketball coach at Farley High took a look at Angel and figured he was just the kid to make his dream of a state championship a reality. Angel was athletic, and smart as a whip, and sure 'nuff, during his senior year, Farley High School became Kentucky state champions for the first time in the school's history. And then Angel got hisself a scholarship to college, went to law school and passed the bar exam with flying colors.

"The town was right proud of their young lawyer.

"Angel married a girl from across the mountain named Sara Beth Moody and they had one son—Delmore. That's when the hoopla started. Angel was set on giving his son everything he had done without, and spoiled Delmore plumb rotten. It was so bad that no one could stand to be around him, not even his mother.

One day, she got in the passenger seat of a F-150 belonging to a coal executive and never looked back.

"If it bothered Angel, he didn't show it. He had Delmore and his law practice and that was all he needed.

"Delmore wasn't the athlete his daddy was, and what with his bad attitude and ornery nature, he was in and out of trouble during high school. But he did have his daddy's brains and his money, so off to college he went. He come back to Farley a few years later with a engineering degree and a job offer from Appalachian Mining.

"Delmore was older, but he wasn't none wiser. He was still the same spoiled boy and before long he was cutting corners, pushing the men and the equipment too hard.

"In a mine you gotta worry about the gas level getting too high and causing an explosion. In the old days they used a canary. Now they have a sensor that sends an alarm so you know to cut everything off and let it vent. Every now and then you'll find a manager that doesn't let anyone know 'cause it means he'd have to stop production. Delmore was like that. The explosion killed eight men.

"There was a long investigation, and when it was over, Appalachian Mining blamed Delmore. At the trial, some folks claimed Delmore had unhooked the sensor and told the men to keep working. Jail seemed likely, but then the judge called a mistrial and the case was dismissed. Folks 'round here said Angel bribed the judge.

"That weekend Delmore took his car to town to celebrate his winning. They found it in a heap at the bottom of Wilder Mountain, with Delmore dead as a doornail. After that, Angel just gave up. Closed his business and moved back to the empty shack where he'd grown up."

"Wow. How long ago did this happen?" Gilbert asked.

Gran scratched her nose, thinking. "Eleven or twelve years ago, I reckon."

"Around the time you were born, Wavie, so it makes sense," Camille said. "Your case must have been one of the last ones he did."

"I sure don't like the thought of going up there to ask him," I said.

"Ask him what?" Gran asked.

"Wavie thinks he might have handled something for her mama," Camille said.

"Well, if he did, I'd chance the asking. Lord knows that man used to love to yammer. He had enough tongue for six rows of teeth."

"See, Wavie," Gilbert said. "He's probably bored up there by himself. You just have to get him started."

"Sounds to me like you have it figured out," I said. "I'll wait here with Gran and you two go!"

"This thing you want to know," Gran said. "How important is it?"

Camille and Gilbert turned to stare at me. I sighed. "Pretty important."

Gran grinned her crooked smile. "Then it seems to me you're burning daylight, girl. Good luck."

GRAN MIGHT HAVE thought time was wasting, but I was in a different frame of mind. I'd already been toe-to-stinky-toe with Angel, and starting a conversation with him was something I'd have to do at my own pace. Plus, I wanted to plant some flowers on Delmore's grave first. If someone planted flowers by Mama's plaque, I'd tell them anything they wanted to know and then some.

I separated a clump of Shasta daisies I'd found growing behind Gilbert's trailer. They'd do nicely at the cemetery, and there was a spot by the back door of Samantha Rose's house that could use some color.

The kitchen had plenty of dishes to hold the transplanted flowers. I pulled a handful of large plastic bowls out from under the cabinet. Everything was upside down to keep the bugs out, but I washed them anyway. Even plant roots deserved a bug-free beginning.

"'Sup, nerd?" Hoyt stomped into the kitchen and jerked open the refrigerator door. He pulled a milk carton out and shook it. "This is empty." He glared his mean eyes at me. "I thought Mama said to stay out of it!"

"I do my milk drinking at school," I said. "Uncle Philson had cereal twice today." I should know; I had washed both of his bowls.

Hoyt threw the carton across the room and into the trash can. "I hate this house." He stomped over to the pantry and pulled out a Kool-Aid packet. "Give me some water."

I turned on the tap and filled a pitcher, then handed it to him.

He poured the Kool-Aid in and mixed it with his finger, then took a long drink from the spout.

I was pretty sure the image of his dirty purple fingernail would haunt me forever. "Samantha Rose threw some of your jeans in the wash with mine. I put them on the stairs."

Hoyt licked a trail of grape Kool-Aid off his wrist. "Good. Wash my baseball pants, too. I need them for a game."

I put my thumb and pinkie up to my ear like a phone. "Wavie's Laundromat is closed. Sorry."

He leaned forward, his greasy patch of hair just inches from my face. Teenage boys are gross up close and personal. He smelled like grape Kool-Aid and feet.

"Did you moo something? I don't speak cow."

"Samantha Rose didn't say anything about me doing your laundry, Hoyt."

He grabbed my hand and turned it upside down, bending my fingers back.

"*Oww!*"

"My baseball pants. And my socks. Got it?"

"Yes!" I said, wincing. It took everything I had not to cry but I wouldn't give him the satisfaction.

I held my palm against my stomach after he stomped off, and tried flexing my fingers. I was going to do everything I could to leave this place, even if it meant visiting a smelly half-baked hermit like Angel Davis.

CHAPTER TWENTY-FOUR

Samantha Rose's house was a dump, but it was a palace compared to the shack where Angel lived. We peered through the thick brush and I pointed to the side of the house. A clothesline hanging between two rusty poles held a bedsheet and a red long-sleeved shirt. "He does laundry. That's normal, right?"

"Yeah, completely," Gilbert said. "So what's the plan?"

"We'll go into the yard and yell hello from a respectable distance," I suggested.

"What's a respectable distance?" Gilbert asked.

"Far enough away you can breathe over the stink," I said.

"Then what?"

"That's as far as I got."

Gilbert's hair was getting long and he flicked it out of his face. "Did you plant the flowers on Delmore's grave?"

"Yeah," I said. "But I don't know if he's noticed yet. It's only been two days."

"Everybody knows everything in Convict Holler."

"Then why'd you ask if I planted them?"

"Good point!" Gilbert said. He shook his head. "Angel don't have anything better to do. He knows."

"Wavie's going to graduate before we get this over," Camille said. "Are you ready or not?"

"Not. But let's go anyway." I moved from behind the bush and walked to the edge of the clearing. Angel Davis's house loomed in front of me. The sun had moved lower in the sky and everything was bathed in a soft gold.

"Hello!" I shouted. Even though my run-ins with Angel hadn't been bad, unless you counted the stink of a thousand dirty socks soaked in the carcass of a sewer rat as bad, I was still scared—especially approaching him on his property. I could hear Gilbert and Camille breathing heavy beside me.

It seemed like forever, but the wooden door slowly opened and Angel Davis walked out onto the porch.

"I'm pretty sure I just tooted," Gilbert whispered.

"Good afternoon," Camille called. "We came to talk to you."

He glared at us from the porch. "What about?" he yelled.

I clasped my hands in front of me to stop them from shaking. "It's about my mama, Ronelda Conley."

For a second he didn't react, then he shuffled toward the end of the porch. "Ronelda. Right."

"So you knew her?" I asked.

Angel nodded. "Of course I knew her!" He folded himself onto a metal chair. He rested his long arms on top of his knees. I thought he looked like a very old, very hairy Daddy Long Legs.

"What about the rest of you. Who's your kin?" Angel asked.

"I'm Effie Miller's grandson," Gilbert said. He pointed to Camille. "Her family just moved here a couple of years ago."

"A-huh," he grunted. A few long seconds passed as he stared at us. "Well," he yelled, "get on with it! I make three hundred dollars an hour, you're costing money."

We exchanged confused glances. "Okay," I said. "Do you remember helping my mom put a baby up for adoption?"

"Adoptions?" he said loudly. "I don't do those now. Too much trouble."

"No, sir," I said. "It's about an adoption you did about eleven years ago. For my mom, Ronelda."

"Ronelda. Right. Of course I knew her!"

Gilbert shook his head. "This conversation has more circles than the Daytona 500."

I took a step closer and tried again. "Did you help Ronelda put her baby up for adoption? To a woman named Anita Bowman?"

Angel nodded his head without speaking.

"I think he's going to sleep," Camille whispered.

"*Yes!*" Angel yelled. "No, wait." He rubbed his beard. "We had a problem with that one."

"That's right," I said. "The adoption didn't go through."

"It didn't." He looked at me. "You placed your baby, then all the trouble started and you changed your mind. How's your baby?"

I moved up onto the porch until I was standing next to Angel, which, considering the smell of him, was no easy thing. "She's fine. Thanks for asking."

His eyes cleared for a moment. "You planted daisies on Delmore's grave."

"Yes." I swallowed hard. "I lost my mama, too, remember?"

Gilbert and Camille came to stand on the porch steps.

"You said trouble?" Gilbert asked. "What kind of trouble?"

Angel stretched his knee out. "The dad's people got involved. It's always the way." He pointed a long bony finger at me. "But you didn't let them get her, did you?"

"No," I said softly. "They didn't get her."

"You done good, just wanting the best for your baby girl."

"Yes," I said. "Thank you. For helping."

He just sat and stared without moving as we left the yard.

IT WAS SHAME-A-LOT day and the Farley Middle School cafeteria was wilder than a shopping mall the week before Christmas. Frank and Beans were chasing two fourth-graders, homework was being passed back and forth, and tired teachers were gossiping over their coffee cups in the corner.

Camille hurried into the room and sat down. "I'm starving. Can I have a bite of your muffin?"

I handed it over. "What took you so long?"

"Mrs. Rivers wasn't exactly thrilled to let me go to the library by myself. I think she has trust issues."

Gilbert nodded. "She hugged me extra-long today. You get lice once and they never let you forget it."

"Did you find out anything?" I asked.

"Oh yeah! That registry website is full of information. Kentucky gives the birth mom ten days to change her mind, right? But if there's any other trouble during that time, say another family member steps in or something, then the adoptive family becomes foster parents until the whole thing gets settled."

"So technically I've already been in foster care?"

"If Angel had the story straight," Camille said.

"That's a big if," Gilbert said. "Angel don't have both oars in the water on a good day."

"I've been adopted, in foster care and an orphan all by the age of eleven," I grumbled. "Did I break a mirror in the delivery room or something? That's some streak of bad luck."

"Why didn't those Bowman people just keep her as a foster kid?" Gilbert asked.

"I don't know for sure," Camille said, "but one of the commenters on the site said the family would have probably won out over a foster situation."

I leaned back in my chair. "Mama placed me for adoption, then my dad's family butts in, so my mom took me back to keep them from getting me?"

"That's what it seems like to me," Camille said.

"Mama always said that other than my daddy, his family was born sorry. But at least they wanted me."

Camille plopped her backpack on the table and pulled out her notebook. "And so did the Bowmans. Now you can write your letter."

As much as I hated the idea, the Bowmans were step one of Operation Escape. "I'll write them, but I am not asking them to take me in like some stray poodle."

"You're more like a collie," Gilbert said. "Long hair, goofy grin."

"And you're like a flea aggravating me to death!"

"Whatever you want," Camille said. She handed me a pen.

"Good. 'Cause if I do this, then Gilbert has to try to get in the GT classes."

Gilbert's head jerked backward like he'd been hit with a two-by-four. "How'd I get tangled into this?"

"If I'm doing something, you're doing something."

Gilbert pointed to Camille. "What about her? What does she have to do?"

I drummed my fingers on the table, thinking. "She has to teach Frank and Beans to read."

"What?" Camille yelled. "I don't have time to do my own homework."

"You're the one that said they could read if someone cared enough to teach them. And we all have to start calling them Frank and Baily, no more Beans."

Camille rolled her eyes. "Fine, start writing."

"Gilbert?" I asked. "You'll actually try to get in to GT?"

"Sure, yeah, why not," he said. "Maybe I'll get lucky and flunk."

I picked up the pen again and after thinking for a few seconds, scribbled a short note. I slid it in front of them.

Dear Anita,

Wavie found your name in my papers and is asking lots of questions about what happened. What do you think I should tell her?

Ronelda

"I agreed to GT classes for that?" Gilbert said. "You didn't even tell them it was you!"

"They might be crazy," I said. "I want to feel them out some first."

Camille folded the paper and stuck it in her bag. "I'll get a stamp from my dad. Now we just have to figure out how to keep the answer out of Samantha Rose's grubby fingers."

"Why don't we use one of your addresses?" I asked.

"Gran makes Flipper Johnson hand the mail directly to her. She's not about to lose her Social Security check to one of the two-bit thieves around here." Gilbert's neck flushed tomato red. "No offense, Wavie."

"It'd be suspicious to put our names on it," Camille said. "And if you put our address, Flipper will think it's a mistake and put it in your mailbox anyway."

The warning bell rang and chairs scraped across the tile floor as a hundred pairs of legs began to scurry off to class.

"Samantha Rose's box is with everybody else's at the bottom of the hill," I said. "We'll just have to be down there every day before she is."

We figured that if I started bringing in the mail every day, Samantha Rose would grow suspicious, so we decided to take turns waiting on Flipper Johnson. Since we never knew when he'd show up, Camille enlisted Frank and Baily to help watch, too. As soon as the mail truck disappeared out of sight, one of us would pop up from behind the row of mailboxes, check for a letter from the Bowmans, then stuff everything back inside.

"It's been a week already," Gilbert said. "Are you sure we sent it to the right address?"

"Maybe they're on vacation and didn't get it," Camille said.

"Or maybe they know Mama is dead," I said, "and don't want any part of me."

Whatever the reason, the Bowmans weren't writing back. Operation Escape was a dud.

CHAPTER TWENTY-FIVE

I wrung the water out of my jeans and hung them on the clothes-line. I'd already taken down and folded a load of towels, ugly Hoyt's ugly ball pants and Samantha Rose's undergarments. "If we ever need to make a sail, I know whose underwear to use," I said to Spotted One. His tail thumped against the ground as I scratched behind his ear. "There's half a piece of bologna coming your way after dinner."

Samantha Rose's Buick bounced and shimmied up the road and pulled to a stop with a hiss. She climbed out holding a Walmart bag in each hand. "You pick up the living room?"

"Yes."

"What about Philson? He get his snack?"

"I gave him some cereal, no milk, like you said."

Samantha Rose nodded. "Here." She threw the two bags to me.

"What's this?"

"They ain't Chinese puzzle boxes. Open them up and see for yourself."

I squatted down in the grass and opened the bags. One held a pair of jeans and a short-sleeve shirt that bore a map of Kentucky with the words *The Bluegrass State* written under it. The other bag had a pair of new sneakers.

"These are for me?"

"No, they're for Hoyt. Of course they're for you," Samantha Rose said. "Run put them on. And go wash your face while you're at it."

I went into the kitchen. It still looked shabby, but not like the day I'd first arrived. As I walked down the hallway to my room, I noticed lots of differences. The pictures on the wall in the hallway looked better since I'd rearranged them so that Mama had the best spots, eye level. I'd put Samantha Rose on the lower nails.

I tapped the photos of Mama as I passed, baby picture after baby picture, then first grade, second grade, on up until the last one where she was wearing a cap and gown. I stood back and looked at them all: Mama, Samantha Rose, the odd one here and there of my grandparents. "There aren't any baby pictures of Samantha Rose," I said to Mama's seventh-grade photo. "Probably broke the camera."

The living room wasn't nearly as cluttered as it had been the day I'd moved in either. Hoyt had burned all the newspapers and magazines in the backyard, and the knickknacks now sat in neat rows on the shelves. The radio wasn't constantly playing music anymore, but the flat-screen television I'd bought was turned on to a news program. Uncle Philson waved from his spot on the couch, then closed his eyes.

I went into my room and began to put on my new clothes. The jeans were the right size, but I guess I'd lost weight since I'd moved in, and they hung low on my hips. The T-shirt fit, but the shoes were a size too big. I thought about stuffing the toes with toilet paper, but we were down to the last of the roll and I didn't want to waste it.

"Wavie!" Samantha Rose yelled from outside. "Come on out here and let me look at you."

I pushed open the screen door and came down the steps.

"Not bad, not bad." Samantha Rose motioned for me to come closer. I leaned back, bracing for another slap. Instead, she gently pulled the tag off the jeans and put it in her pocket. "Don't get those dirty. They were thirty-two dollars, if you can believe that. I'll take 'em back once the hearing is over."

"When what's over?" I asked, but a familiar car had already turned onto the road and was headed up the hill.

Mrs. Chipman was finally here.

MRS. CHIPMAN HUGGED me hard and long. "Girl, I swear you are a sight for sore eyes."

I lingered, my face pressed against her blouse. Mrs. Rivers and her lice check/high five was nice, but it couldn't compete with Mrs. Chipman's full-on hug.

She put her arm around my shoulders. "That's quite a house. When was it built?"

Samantha Rose was wearing her special-occasion leopard

again. "Early 1900s. I know it don't look like much to city people, but we like the peace and quiet."

"I can understand that." She looked toward the backyard. "Are those train tracks?"

"Yes," I said. I looked at my watch. "The coal train will be by in about an hour. If we're in the backyard he'll blow his horn."

"Why don't we go in and sit?" Samantha Rose asked, smiling. "I've got some store-bought cake inside."

"Oh, that sounds delightful," Mrs. Chipman said, "but I need a little time with Wavie." She coughed. "Alone."

Samantha Rose's smile lost some of its luster, but she nodded. "Why don't you show Mrs. Chipman around, Wavie? I'll go cut the cake."

My shoes flapped as I walked, and I concentrated on stepping carefully around any wet patches on the path that led to the cemetery. If Samantha Rose wanted to return these, too, she'd be ill if they were mud stained.

"How do you like your new school so far?" Mrs. Chipman asked.

"It's good," I said. "Smaller than Andro, but the kids are really nice."

"And your aunt and uncle? You like living here?"

I hesitated. "It's different."

"I imagine it would be. It's bound to take some getting used to."

We reached the cemetery and sat down on the bench. "What are foster homes like?" I asked Mrs. Chipman.

"Some are better than others. You know I promised your mama I'd do my best to find you a good one." She stared at me, her eyes solemn. "You aren't happy here?"

"Samantha Rose is nothing like my mama," I said. I pulled at a honeysuckle vine that had wound its way up the bench. "If I found somewhere else to go, could I?"

"You mean like with a neighbor?"

"I guess."

Mrs. Chipman moved her head side to side, thinking. "They'd have to petition the court, too. If your aunt decided to fight it, the court usually goes with the family, and she seems like a fighter to me."

"Yeah, she sure is." I looked at the path leading to Angel's house. "What if the people were folks my mom liked better?"

"If your mama had named someone specific, that'd help. But I did ask your mom for names and she didn't give me any."

I sighed. "What if I really hate it here? You'd move me to foster care?"

"I would *recommend* moving you to foster care. I'm not going to sugarcoat it, honey, there are some good foster homes out there. But you're eleven. That's a hard age to place, and we have a shortage of homes. You might be put in a group home for a while." She placed her hand on my arm. "Do you? Hate it here?"

"Sometimes," I answered.

Mrs. Chipman's mouth turned down at the corners. "Tell me the truth, now. Are they abusing you in some way?"

I thought about the slap. I wasn't one hundred percent sure if that qualified. I wasn't sure about anything. If I asked to be moved, I might be giving up Camille and Gilbert for a worse situation. "No," I finally answered.

"Well, that's a load off." She stood up. "So this is a family cemetery?"

"More like a community one. Some of my family is here, but there are others." I smiled. "Gilbert says everything in Convi—uh, Conley Holler is connected."

Mrs. Chipman walked up and down, reading. "Oh, a poor child. Now that's sad. I love that verse, though. Matthew 5:8. 'Blessed are the pure in heart for they will see God.'"

"When's the hearing?" I asked. "That'll make this permanent, right?"

"Once that's done, yes." She tugged at her panty hose. "I'm filing my home visit report on Monday. Then it's just a matter of the judge putting it on his calendar. You want me to look into some foster homes?"

"I don't know. They might be bad, and I don't know for sure if another family is interested. It's all kind of hopeless."

Mrs. Chipman pointed to the gravestones. "Until I'm under one of those, I don't ever stop hoping. You know another verse I love? Jeremiah 29:11. 'For I know the plans I have for you, declares the Lord, plans to prosper you and not to harm you, plans to give you a hope and a future.'"

"That was one Mama used to say." My eyes started to water,

thinking about her. "She said that everybody—rich or poor, it didn't matter—they all had the promise of a hope and a future."

Mrs. Chipman hugged me. "Your mama was a smart woman."

"I don't want you to look for foster homes," I said. "But can you put off the hearing for a little while?"

"I can't put it off forever, but I'll do my best. Okay?"

I nodded.

"Then let's go get some of that store-bought cake."

TWO DAYS AFTER Mrs. Chipman's visit, the letter came.

CHAPTER TWENTY-SIX

It was lying there, a large tan envelope among the grocery circulars and the demand-for-payment bills. I grabbed it to my chest and ran to get Camille and Gilbert.

"Are you going to open it?" Gilbert asked. "Or just stare at it all day."

We were sitting knee to knee in the grass behind Gilbert's trailer. Frank and Baily were in the distance trying unsuccessfully to get a kite off the ground. I knew it was silly, but it seemed like the air around us had stilled in anticipation.

"Go ahead, Wavie," Camille said.

I undid the clasp at the top of the envelope and opened the flap. I pulled out a single sheet of pale blue paper and laid it on the ground.

"It's got their names on it," Gilbert said. "Printed. They really are highfalutin folks, ain't they!"

I nudged it toward Camille. "I'm too nervous. You do it."

"Okay, here goes," she said:

Dear Ronelda,

We were very excited to get your letter. We've been wondering how you are feeling. I hope that this letter finds you in better health.

I'm sorry that Wavie found our checks, although I'm not surprised. How many times have you written that she's bright and curious.

I know this must be hard, but I've always found that what they say is true, honesty is the best policy. I've enclosed a couple of letters that we exchanged that might be helpful. After all of this time, I still have everything. If you think she'd want to see more, let me know and I'll put them in the mail.

Sincerely,

Anita

Camille stuck her arm into the light. "I've got chills. Seriously, look!"

Gilbert snorted. "I think it's weird. 'I hope that this letter finds you in better health'? No one around here talks like that. Did your mama send you to the Queen of England?"

I tilted the envelope and poured the contents onto the grass. There were two more letters and a photograph.

"Wavie, look! Is this you?" Camille picked up a photo showing two people and a baby.

"I guess so. It looks a little bit like one of the JCPenney portraits I have in a drawer at Samantha Rose's."

"Let me see," Gilbert said. He turned the photo toward him. "You can tell they're city people."

Up until then I'd been staring at my own bald head and hadn't paid much attention to the Bowmans. Gilbert was right. They were definitely shiny. Both of them had thick dark hair and big toothy smiles. They looked like they ought to be on the side of a toothpaste box. The woman had tilted the baby forward so that whoever was taking the photo could see her face. I looked like an alien next to them.

Camille picked up the top sheet of paper. "Hey, this is the birth mother letter."

"What's that?" I asked.

"Remember my cousin Petra, in Texas? Mama said the adoptive parents had to write a letter to the birth mom so she could choose who she wanted—this must be the one the Bowmans sent your mom. Want me to read it, too?"

I nodded. "This is so weird."

"'Dear Birth Mother,'" Camille began:

> *We are honored that you are taking the time to consider us*
> *as an adoptive family and want to tell you a little about us.*
> *I am a fifth-grade math teacher, but plan on being a stay-*
> *at-home mom when I become a mother.*

"A math teacher," Gilbert said. "They're the worst."

"Shh," Camille said. She continued:

> *While teaching keeps me busy, I do find some time*
> *occasionally to paint, spend time with my friends, and*
> *participate in church activities. My husband, John, is*
> *an attorney and we have been blessed this year in that*
> *we have been able to buy our first house. It's a modest*
> *three bedroom, but it is in a very safe neighborhood.*
>
> *We enjoy our time together. During the summer*
> *we spend weekends boating, hiking or fishing.*

Camille turned the paper around. "Look, here's a picture of them in a canoe. Nice!"

I leaned forward for a better look. The photo showed the two of them in plaid shirts and jeans, holding a tiny fish and smiling like they'd just won the Bassmaster Classic.

Gilbert snorted. "Is that the fish or the bait?"

I closed my eyes and listened as Camille continued:

> *During the winter, we enjoy skiing, and try to get*
> *away to the mountains as much as possible.*

"Seriously. Don't they seem kind of braggy?" Gilbert asked.

Camille ignored him.

We have always dreamed of having a family, and
being able to adopt would be a dream come true. We
hope that you will consider us and you have our word
that we would do everything possible to give your baby a
wonderful life.

Sincerely,
John and Anita Bowman

Camille handed me the letter. "They look like the same people in the photo."

"I guess so," I said. It felt beyond crazy. I had lived with those people. They were almost my parents! "We know I was almost adopted, but I still don't know why."

Camille picked up the other letter and handed it to me. "Maybe this one will tell us more. It's from your mom."

I stared at Mama's handwriting, the crossed *t*'s, the loops and swirls of the letters, and a pain speared my chest so hard it was all I could do not to cry out.

"You want me to keep going?"

I shook my head. "I'll do it."

My voice quivered as I began to read:

Dear Anita,

Thank you for writing. Mr. Davis said once the
adoption was final you could send pictures twice a
year. I'd like that. I hope they are pictures of her doing

fun things like riding horses or going to Disney. Not
when she's a baby of course, but one day. It's a funny
thing, but I've never met one person who's actually
been to Disney World. Then again most folks I know
never been out of Kentucky. The day I found out I was
pregnant I was in the hospital getting blood work done.
I was staring out the window, watching all the traffic
on 85, and wondering where they were all heading. The
nurse said it was spring break and that as soon as her
shift was over she was going to be right there with them
on her way to Florida. I was thinking about Florida and
what it would be like to stick my feet in the sand and
feel the waves, when the doctor came in with the news
I was pregnant. I've been calling her Wavie in my head
ever since. I knew she was a girl way before the nurse
that did the ultrasound said so. Do you have a name
picked out? Maybe it's best that I don't know. Then I'd
start thinking of her in concrete fashion. Wavie reminds
me of the beach and other things I'll never know. It will
make things easier I believe.

I took a deep breath. My eyes were full of tears and I needed a
second for them to clear enough to see to keep reading:

Anyway, I'm doing my best to take care of her while
she's here. I've been eating as much fruit and vegetables as
I can get ahold of and I won't let anyone smoke near us.

Good luck with your painting. It sounds like the
nursery is coming along real nice. If you wanted to send
a picture of her room, I'd like to see it. Don't feel obliged.
I just wanted you to know I'm okay with hearing about
her future life.

Sincerely,
Ronelda M. Conley

"Did you know that about your name?" Gilbert asked.

"Not all of it," I whispered. "I knew she'd been thinking about Florida when she found out about me, but that's all."

The afternoon coal train rumbled by and I felt the soft vibrations through the ground. Ever since Mama had died, life had felt like this, uneven and off balance. I picked up the photograph and looked at it again. "It settles one thing. There's no way I'm going to ask them to take me back."

"What? Why not?" Camille asked.

I stuffed the letters and the picture back in the envelope. "I'd fit in with those people about as much as a skunk at a garden party. Did you see the man's hair? He looks like someone on TV that gives the weather!"

Gilbert nodded. "Yep. They've got raised on concrete written all over them. Probably got a house full of stuck-up kids by now, too."

"Can you see me canoeing around with those people?" I asked. "The whole thing is crazy."

"Ain't nobody in Convict Holler got common ground with folks like that," Gilbert said.

"You're not helping, Gilbert!" Camille crossed her arms and glared at us. "They sound like normal people. What did you want them to be like, Wavie?"

"I don't know," I said, shrugging. "Better than sorry, but not rich."

"What's wrong with rich?" Camille said. "Haven't either one of you ever seen *Annie*?"

Gilbert moved to the side and stretched out in the grass. "Rich people don't care anything about people like us."

"What about the Farley Methodist ladies? Don't you get a backpack full of food from them every Friday?" Camille asked.

"That's how they feel good about themselves," Gilbert said.

"They give poor kids food." She pretended to shudder. "The monsters!"

"They might not be monsters," Gilbert said, "but everybody knows you can't trust rich people."

Camille threw up her hands. "I don't get it. You want to get out of Convict Holler, too, Gilbert, but you don't like people with money? Where you planning on going?" Camille asked.

"I ain't got it all figured out yet," Gilbert said. "But I won't be depending on rich people to get me there."

I listened, nodding my head occasionally. I mostly agreed with Gilbert. The girls that came from money at my last school walked around with their noses so far up in the air they'd drown in a hard rain. But Mama had chosen the Bowmans especially. She had to have had good reasons.

Camille looked at me. "Are you afraid that you won't fit in with them, or that they'll say no?"

"Both, I guess. You wouldn't understand."

"I might." She played with her necklace. "Don't freak out, but my parents are thinking of sending me to private school."

Gilbert sat up. "What? You're leaving, too?"

"I wouldn't be leaving, just going to a different school. But I know how you're feeling, Wavie. Sort of, anyway," Camille said. "Where's your mama's letter?"

"You put it back in the envelope."

"No, the other letter. The one you carry around with you all of the time with your mama's final instructions."

"Oh," I said. "Up at the house."

"What does number six say, and don't even try to pretend you can't remember."

I sighed. "'Be brave, Wavie B.! You got as much right to a good life as anybody, so find it!'"

"Exactly, *be brave*. Write them again and ask for one of the other letters Mrs. Bowman mentioned. It can't hurt."

"Ask her something about her house," Gilbert said. "I bet rich ladies love to talk about decorating and stuff like that."

"One more letter," I said. "And then, whatever I decide, you guys have to be okay with it. Deal?"

Camille crossed her heart. "Deal."

I picked up the envelope and stood. "I've got to get back be-fore Samantha Rose starts looking for me. Since she bought the new TV, I'm in charge of dinner."

"You mean since *you* bought the new TV," Camille said.

"Any word on the hearing?" Gilbert asked.

"No, but she wouldn't tell me anyway. I won't know till she stuffs me in the Buick and heads to town."

"Be brave, Wavie B.," Camille said. "Write your letter."

CHAPTER TWENTY-SEVEN

My shoe connected with the plastic bottle with a satisfying thunk. It flew, end over end, up the dusty road another six feet.

Mama and Camille had said *be brave* like it was no big deal. I moved forward and kicked the bottle again. The tip of my white sneaker scraped the dirt, turning it gray, and I squatted down to clean it off.

I hesitated, my hand hovering over the dirty canvas. A brave girl wouldn't care what Samantha Rose said about returning her clothes, not when they were the only ones she had that fit—and that she herself had paid for!

I took a deep breath and swirled my fingers into the dirt, then ran them across the front of my shoe. Four dark streaks stood out against the gleaming white. I dipped my fingers again, this time drawing them across my jeans. Samantha Rose would probably have a hissy fit when she saw what I'd done. "Not much daylight between being brave and being stupid if you ask me," I grumbled.

As if just thinking of Samantha Rose made her appear, she stepped out onto the porch and slammed the door. "Hey! What are you doing lolling about in the middle of the road," she yelled.

My heart skipped a beat. Surely she couldn't see my clothes from up there. I grabbed the soda bottle. "Picking up litter," I yelled back.

She walked to the Buick. "Well, get out of the way. I'm heading to town and you make a poor speed bump."

I was almost to the yard by the time she reversed the car out of the weeds and sped off down the drive.

Hoyt had left earlier, off somewhere with Zane, which meant it would just be me and Uncle Philson in the house. We hadn't had another conversation since he'd settled the question of whether my dad was actually dead, but there was one more thing I wanted to know.

I hadn't told Camille or Gilbert, but before I wrote to the Bowmans, I wanted to rule out my dad's family as a possible alternative. Sorry or not, they might want to know me.

B-R-A-V-E G-I-R-L—GIVER, VIABLE, LIVE. A brave girl would want to know the truth. I opened the screen door and hurried inside.

MY UNCLE WAS always in one of three places: his bedroom sleeping, the kitchen eating, or in his recliner listening to country music. I followed the sound of Dolly Parton's "Jolene" to the living room.

As usual, he lay horizontal, feet in the air with his eyes closed.

I'd been in the room to clean, but I'd never sat in there. I looked for a clean spot between the stains on the couch and sat down. The cushion made a *pffft* sound, and the smell of something spoiled and moldy floated around me.

Uncle Philson opened his eyes, blinking as if he'd been dreaming and now had no idea where he was. "Samantha!"

I shook my head. "She left five minutes ago."

He yawned, then pulled the lever on the recliner and sat up. The sweet voice of Dolly had turned into that of a car salesman, and he motioned for me to turn the radio off.

Sitting there in his sock feet, he looked sallow and weak. I tried to imagine him going to work every day, digging coal out of a mine, but it was impossible. I could be brave in the face of Uncle Philson. "You said my dad was dead."

He wiped his eyes and yawned again. "What?"

"You said my dad was dead. What about his family?"

"What about them?" he asked.

I traced the outline of a purple stain. The thought of being in this house and watching Hoyt suck down grape Kool-Aid for the rest of my life was too depressing. "Are any of them still around? In Farley or near about, I mean?"

"Jud's people? I think he has a brother what's not in jail." He pulled his sock down and scratched his ankle where tiny blue veins collided. "I wouldn't swear by it, though. I seen all of them wearing orange vests and picking up trash at some point."

It shouldn't have bothered me—Mama had said they weren't worth knowing—but it did. I sagged against the back of the couch. Being brave was tiring. No wonder everybody in Conley Holler looked faded and worn out. I pushed myself off the couch and stood.

Uncle Philson flipped the lever on his recliner and leaned back. "Radio!"

I turned the volume back up and shuffled down the hall.

I SAT IN my room at the desk, running my fingers along the dents and scratches. I liked to pretend that they were made by Mama when she was a girl.

I needed to write a letter.

I needed to write a letter to the people who had almost been my family.

I needed to write a letter that would be so good, they'd write back and I'd know if living with them was even a possibility.

There was no way that I was going to be able to do that, so instead I sat at the desk and did everything else *but* write the letter. I flipped through Mama's worn New Testament. I blew kisses to Mama's picture. I opened the drawer and pulled out the other photographs I'd brought from our trailer and laid them on top of the desk.

I stared at the framed 8x10 from the JCPenney Portrait Studios. It was made when I was six months old. "I was still bald," I said to Mama's picture. "Why would you tape a bow to my head?"

I held the photo up and looked closer. The dress was short,

revealing my pudgy legs that ended in lace-trimmed socks and patent-leather shoes.

Samantha Rose had returned an hour ago. She and Uncle Philson were now sitting in front of the television, but I got up and locked the door anyway.

I pulled the envelope from Anita Bowman out from under my mattress and dug around until I found the picture of the three of us. No wonder the dress in the portrait was so short. It was the very same one I was wearing with the Bowmans.

I blew my bangs out of my eyes. If I'd stayed with them, everything would have been different. And I wouldn't have known Mama, Camille or Gilbert.

Samantha Rose cackled from the other room and I felt my stomach roil. Our neighbor back home at Castle Fields Mobile Home Park had an old bird dog named Festus. One day he stopped in our yard and began bucking and gagging and basically having a fit. Mama watched from the lawn chair she'd pulled underneath a skinny tree made from an out-of-control juniper bush.

What is that fool dog doing? she'd asked.

By the time I ran over, Festus had puked a slimy green mixture onto a bald patch of dirt. In the middle was a peach pit as big as a tobacco can. Hard and greasy. That's what the knot in my stomach felt like every time I looked at Samantha Rose.

If I'd stayed with the Bowmans, I would have never known her either.

I sat back down at the desk and looked at the photo of Mama.

"I don't care," I whispered. "I wouldn't trade having you as my mom for anything. Samantha Rose is terrible, but it's a price I'm willing to pay for my time with you."

Be brave, Mama had said. I put my notebook on the desk and picked up a pen.

> *Dear Anita,*
>
> *Thank you for writing back. Wavie is glad that she stayed with me, but she has so many questions about y'all. You know how kids are. She said she wouldn't have fit in with you anyway, she doesn't canoe or hike, and math is her worst subject. Do you think she would have, really? Your letter talked about your house. Have you done anything new to it? I'd love to hear all about your renovations. Also, if you could send any of those other letters you mentioned, that'd be great.*
>
> *Your friend,*
> *Ronelda*

I reread it trying to hear it in Mama's voice. It didn't sound like her; she wouldn't have cared a bit about their house, but I didn't know what else to say. I shoved the note into my backpack.

It would work or it wouldn't.

We'd know soon.

CHAPTER TWENTY-EIGHT

Maybe it was spring having finally decided to send the last of the cool temperatures packing that made me feel hopeful as I walked to the bus stop. I breathed in the smell of pine and honeysuckle. Rows and rows of mountain ridges were etched against the sky as far as I could see. They were deep green up close, but the morning haze turned them lighter and lighter until nothing but a faint silver silhouette remained in the distance.

Frank and Baily were staring at Camille like she had two heads. "You called me Baily," Baily said, grinning. "No take backs."

"I don't want to take it back. Tell the kids in your class I said to stop it, too. If they have a problem, they can see me."

Gilbert hitched his sweatpants higher. "Go on, tell them the rest of it."

"After school, come over," Camille said. "I'm going to help you learn to read."

Frank shook his head. "What for?"

"'Cause you need to know. And you're going to make good grades so your mama can see how smart you are. You got it?"

The two of them looked at each other and shrugged. "Okay?"

I smiled at Camille. "Now doesn't that make you feel good?"

"It feels like I'm going to have less time for my own homework is what it feels like."

"You?" Gilbert asked. "Studying to get into GT means I'll have less time for actual cool stuff, like exploring."

Camille rolled her eyes. "What about you, Wavie? Did you write the letter?"

Mr. Vic pulled to a stop, sending gravel hopping, and we climbed aboard. I passed the letter over the back of the seat so Camille could mail it for us. She and Gilbert quickly read it.

"I don't know," Camille said. "You don't really ask much. How are you going to know if they're looking for more kids?"

"What kind of question do you imagine me asking," I said, "that wouldn't make my mama sound like she was two sandwiches short of a picnic?"

"I'm with Wavie," Gilbert said. He smelled his underarm. "Sniff this and tell me if I stink."

"Gross!" Camille said. "Not in this lifetime."

I sat back down and faced the front of the bus. If I stayed in Convict Holler, I'd have to put up with Samantha Rose and Hoyt, but I'd have Gilbert and Camille. I played with a hole in the knee of my jeans. Even if the Bowmans took me in they'd just be doing it out of pity, and then I'd be away from my friends. They'd probably send me to Snob Middle School where everyone would look down on me. When another letter came from them, I might just throw it away without opening it.

THE FIVE OF US took turns checking the mailbox. Friday, it was my turn. I'd had to finish my homework and my chores first and I'd arrived at the bottom of the hill in time to see the back end of the mail truck. He had raised such a cloud of dust that I didn't see the woman standing by the boxes until she moved.

Frank and Baily's mother, the angular Mrs. Barnes, stood there blinking in the sun like she'd just left a dark cave.

"Afternoon," I said.

Mrs. Barnes nodded. "How you?" Her voice was soft as a duck's tail feather.

"Good." I opened the mailbox, but other than some junk mail, there was nothing. I had turned to leave when Mrs. Barnes stopped me.

"The boys told me Camille is learnin' them to read."

I nodded. "Yes, ma'am. She said they're picking it up fairly quickly."

"That's what she told me. I stopped by there to say thank you and she said it was all your idea."

I could feel my face turning red. "I doubt they're too happy with me. Camille is giving them homework."

"They don't seem too bothered." She looked toward Samantha Rose's house. "It's good to see Mrs. Conley's flowers around the place again. I've got a few in my yard that she gave me if you ever want a cutting."

"That would be great. I still haven't been able to find her peony bush."

"There used to be one in the side yard," Mrs. Barnes said, "but I think there's an old car parked there now." She moved forward to stand next to me. "I wanted to tell you I knew your mama. You look just like her."

"You did?" I felt my heart leap. "You knew her from when she lived here?"

"That's right. She was a couple of years ahead of me in school, but we played together some when we was little." She looked toward the house on the hill. "Whenever things got real bad over there, she'd come spend the night." She shook her head and smiled at me. "She was a real good person. I'd heard she was sick. The second I saw you I knew she'd done passed over."

My mouth went dry like it did anytime someone mentioned Mama dying and I felt the familiar hot tears starting to gather in the corners of my eyes. "Why when you saw me?"

Mrs. Barnes smiled sadly. "I knew she wouldn'ta brung you back here if there'd been any strength left in her body."

"Did you know my dad, too?" I asked.

"I knew of him, but Ronelda and I weren't close by high school. But I saw her when she come back for Mrs. Conley's funeral. She told me about you. She was happy she got a better life for you. I know people think I don't want my boys to learn 'cause of the money. It's not true. I want them to find a better life, too." She gave another small smile and began to walk the dusty road toward their house.

The train whistled as it came around the curve and I watched as Frank and Baily raced for the tracks. The ping of their rocks hitting the metal mingled with their laughter and floated down the hollow.

There were hard things about Convict Holler, like living with Samantha Rose. But there was so much beauty here, too. And kind people that I would miss.

CHAPTER TWENTY-NINE

The second letter came on Tuesday and it was a pure miracle that I got it and Samantha Rose didn't. I'd been watching for Flipper Johnson but then Gran yelled that she'd just pulled some biscuits out of the oven and they were so much better if you ate them hot. So I did. Four times. By the time I finally headed to the group of mailboxes at the bottom of the road, I saw three things.

Angel Davis.

Samantha Rose.

The end of a large tan envelope sticking out of the mailbox.

"You need to get back up the mountain, old man!" Samantha Rose said. "You stink."

"Your daddy told me to take care of you," Angel said. "You were supposed to be together with your sister!"

"You're tetched in the head!" Samantha Rose yelled back.

While Samantha Rose and Angel yelled, I moved to the mailbox. If Samantha Rose got ahold of the letter first, there'd be a Wavie B. Conley headstone added to the cemetery.

I tugged on the envelope. It came out, bringing everything else with it, and landed in the dirt.

Samantha Rose whirled around. "What are you doing?"

"I dropped the mail," I said. I hunkered over the strewn envelopes. A grocery circular lay in the middle of everything and I folded it around the envelope from the Bowmans.

"Get it off the ground, for crying out loud."

I stood, hugging the mail against my shirt. "Hi Angel," I said. "What were you saying about my grandpa?"

Angel scratched his beard. "I remember her father!" He towered over Samantha Rose like a giant insect. "I remember him. He told me to take care of her!"

Samantha Rose moved forward until she was nose to thorax with Angel.

I gawked. She had to be crazy furious to get that close to him and the cloud of stink.

"I'm gonna call the county on you, old man," she yelled. "You're a danger to yourself and you stink to high heaven! There's no telling what kind of disease you're spreading in the Holler." She turned back to me and put her hand out. "Give me my mail."

I handed her the stack of envelopes, but held on to the circular. "Flipper put Mrs. Barnes's mail in our mailbox by mistake. I'll run it over to her."

"It's junk. Save yourself the trouble and throw it away."

"I can't," I said. "That's a federal offense!"

She threw her hands up. "I'm surrounded by crazy people," Samantha Rose said. "Suit yourself, but don't stay gone all day."

IN CASE SAMANTHA Rose was watching, I walked toward Frank and Baily's house, and then doubled back through the woods and up to the cemetery.

I went inside the gate and sat down on the cracked bench. The flowers I'd planted were spreading nicely. It was quiet and peaceful.

I ripped the end of the envelope and spilled the contents onto my lap. There were two letters. I picked up the familiar blue stationery and began to read:

> Dear Ronelda,
>
> I don't think you have any idea how excited we were to hear from you. It's been so long, yet we've prayed for you so often these last eleven years, it feels like yesterday. Of course Wavie is glad that she stayed with you! I know how much you love each other.
>
> John laughed when I read to him that Wavie didn't think she'd have fit in. He said, "Babies don't fit in with you. You change everything to fit in with them!" Who knows how raising Wavie would have made our lives different today. She was only here eight days yet it changed us profoundly.
>
> Anyway, that's all water under the bridge. You asked about our house. We still live in the same place. We had the kitchen remodeled last year, and of course we repainted the nursery and turned it into an office, but other than that it's still the same.

I've enclosed the letter that the attorney advised you to write. Maybe it will help Wavie to see what you were thinking about back then.

If there is ever anything we can do for you, please let us know. I'm including my phone number, just in case.

XO,

Anita Bowman

I dropped the Bowman letter on the bench and picked up the other one. Slowly, I unfolded the letter, and gasped. Mama's familiar handwriting was on the first page and it was to me!

Dear Wavie,

You'll be here before I know it and I have so much to tell you.

I lowered the letter. I couldn't do it. It was like Mama was speaking right to me. It was too hard. I closed my eyes and tried to calm down. I wanted to read it so badly, but I was afraid.

Be brave, Mama had said. I opened my eyes. I could do this.

Dear Wavie,

You'll be here before I know it and I have so much to tell you.

Mr. Davis said I should write all of the stuff I want to tell you in a letter for when you're older. The first thing is I love you.

I don't know how old you'll be when you read this but I like to imagine you sitting on your bed—a canopy type with a pink bedspread with ruffles. I saw one like that once at the Lexington Mall and I thought, if I ever have a daughter, that's what she'll have.

You wouldn't have that—or a lot of things—if you were here. That's the second thing I want to tell you. You are better off with your adopted parents than you would be with me.

I ain't going to lie—giving you up was almost more than I could bear. The only way I found the strength was thinking about you and knowing it was the right thing to do. Being strong ain't easy, but if you dig deep enough you can usually find a way. That's my experience, anyhow.

Here are some things I like in case you like them, too, and you wonder where it came from.

Wildflowers.

Strawberries.

The mist that hovers over the mountains in the morning.

There are other things, but those are the top three.

I guess I should tell you about your dad. It's hard to talk about but you deserve to know.

Your dad was a looker and nice as can be. We were crazy about each other but my daddy hated him. Then again, my daddy hated everybody. Maybe if things had been different I wouldn't have decided to find you another family, but before I could tell your dad about you, he was killed in a mining accident.

That was the third thing I wanted to tell you.

I didn't have much schooling but I think if I'd had half a chance I woulda made something of myself. It used to make me sad, all those other people living big lives and me stuck here, but not anymore. Now I get to think about you, living big for the both of us. And that's enough.

The final thing I want to tell you is this. No matter what happens for me or to me from this point on, you are the best thing I ever did. I hope you're happy. But if you have tough days, remember me. If I could be strong, I bet you can, too.

I love you, girl.

          Ronelda May Conley, your mom

I wiped my eyes. I'd felt the loss of Mama every day since she'd been gone, but nothing had hurt as bad as this.

I held my stomach and doubled over, sobbing.

After a few minutes, I stuffed everything back in the envelope and stood. I would do it. I would write the Bowmans, right now before I could change my mind, and ask if I could come back.

CHAPTER THIRTY

I spent the weekend at Camille's writing letters, tearing them up and starting again.

Frank and Baily were at one end of the table practicing their ABCs, while Edgar colored between them.

"How hard can it be?" Gilbert asked. "Just say, 'Congratulations! It's a girl!'"

Camille was more sympathetic. "Keep it simple. Stick to the facts."

"It all sounds right in my head," I said. "But then I put it on paper and it's cuckoo."

Edgar offered me a crayon. "Try writing it in blue, Wavie," he said. "Blue is my favorite."

"No thanks, Edgar."

"It's crazy," Camille said. "Your dad died in a mining accident. You know it was probably the one Delmore Davis caused. Delmore's dad helped your mom. Gilbert is right. Everything in Convict Holler is connected."

"It's like a spiderweb," Gilbert said. "And Samantha Rose is the big fat spider in the middle."

I scribbled another version on the paper.

"How about this?" I read:

Dear Mr. and Mrs. Bowman,

Thank you for writing. I'm sorry, but I wasn't exactly truthful. My mom died recently and I've been staying with my aunt. She wants to be my guardian but I was hoping you'd think on being it instead. My aunt is not very nice. Also, I have my own money, so that wouldn't be a problem. And I would do my best not to cause you any trouble. You don't even have to adopt me, or think of me as a daughter, or anything like that. I had a really good mom and I'm just looking for a decent place that I can call home, even if it's temporary. If yes, could you hurry? The hearing could be any day. If not, I understand.

Wavie Boncil Conley

"I think it sounds great," Camille said. "They'll say yes for sure!"

Gilbert pouted. "Yeah. You'll be sitting in some fancy canoe catching tiny fish before summer's over."

I folded the letter and put it into an envelope. "I wish I had enough money to overnight this. Samantha Rose is being more squirrelly than usual. I've got a feeling the hearing is coming soon and she's not telling me."

"I wouldn't put anything past her," Gilbert said. "She called the county and told them Angel had lost his mind. They took him in for observation!"

I lowered my voice. "Well, he was talking crazy. He kept yelling that my grandpa told him to take care of Samantha Rose."

"He also thought you were your mama, remember?" Camille said. She got up and opened a drawer. "Here's a stamp. Send it as soon as possible. I'll tell Mama to watch the mailboxes while we're at school."

ONE OF US was almost always standing at the mailboxes at the end of the road after I mailed the letter. Flipper Johnson came so close to running over Baily Barnes that he had to sit on the side of the road for an hour before he could drive again because his nerves were so shot. But no letter came for me.

In the mornings, I woke up early to catch the mist that "hovers over the mountains" (Mama was right, it was beautiful) and in the afternoons I picked her favorite wildflowers and arranged them in a Mason jar on my desk.

At night I stayed in my room and tried not to wonder too much about why the Bowmans hadn't written. I imagined them sitting in their kitchen writing down the pros and cons on a sheet of paper. The problem was that when I tried to think of the pros for them, there weren't any.

I pulled out my notepad.

E-I-G-H-T D-A-Y D-A-U-G-H-T-E-R.

DAD.

HEART.

HUG.

There were some good words in that phrase, but who was I kidding. AIRHEAD, DAGGERED, TRAGEDY: those words were there, too. I opened the drawer and pulled out the letter from Mama to read for what had to be the hundredth time.

I could feel how happy she must have been writing it and thinking of me having a good life. If I failed, it would be like letting her down. Now that she was gone, I had to live twice as big.

I turned off the light and lay in bed. I hadn't washed Mama's blanket since I'd been here but I could barely smell the lotion anymore. It was as if she was fading away little by little.

"Mama," I whispered into the room. "I'm trying. I'm trying to be brave and live big, but I don't know if I can." I closed my eyes and imagined her coming into my room and lying down beside me. I could almost feel her hand rubbing my back. "I'm scared the Bowmans won't take me and I'm scared they will." I sighed. "I just miss you so much."

I lay quietly, listening to the sounds of the house. Up above, Hoyt stomped across his room, and the theme song from Samantha Rose's favorite reality show began to play from the living room. I imagined getting up and putting on my jeans. I could see it all in my mind. Walking quietly down the hallway, slipping out the kitchen door, walking into the backyard in the moonlight. I could feel the ground vibrate under my sneakers and I stood there at the curve of the mountain as the train rumbled by. I ran, faster than I'd ever run before. I reached out and grabbed hold of the metal door, then I was up and clinging to the train as we whipped through the trees. I turned around and watched as the light from Samantha Rose's house grew smaller and smaller with each second, and Convict Holler disappeared into the darkness.

Somehow, I'd be flying, free, to wherever the train would take me.

CHAPTER THIRTY-ONE

A week later, I found Samantha Rose waiting for me in the kitchen after school. She wore a smile about as real as her hair color. "Good news! The hearing's been set. In two days, this will be your home for good."

I felt all the blood drain out of my face. "Two days? From now?"

Samantha Rose nodded. "Yup. One o'clock. It'll be good to get it all finalized, won't it?"

No, no, no. This couldn't be happening now. I'd call Mrs. Chipman and stall. "I can't do it on Thursday," I said. "I have a test at school!"

"Bull hockey! That's what makeup tests are for," she said.

"But it's too soon," I blurted. "I need more time."

Samantha Rose sighed. "Let's not do this, okay?" She reached into the front of her shirt and pulled a folded piece of paper out of her bra. I knew it the second I saw the handwriting.

"If you're waiting on an answer to this, it's not coming."

Samantha Rose had taken my letter. It had never even been mailed to the Bowmans.

I stared at my own handwriting. "That's *my* letter!"

"That's right. I saw you put it in the mailbox." She laughed. "You kids have been hovering at those boxes like flies on a cow patty."

"But you have no right! That was my letter!"

"Well, it was in *my* mailbox."

"You're not allowed to take mail out of a mailbox!" I said.

She grabbed my ear and gave it a hard twist. "Who are you to tell me what I can do? You've been writing those people behind my back. After I took you in!"

I jerked my head away and sat down in the nearest chair trying to catch my breath. "You can't stop me from writing them," I said. "Even if I have to do it from school."

Samantha Rose leaned against the sink. "I don't reckon they'll be writing you back anytime soon."

"Why? What are you talking about?"

"Once I realized you were writing them, I figured I better take precautions. I'm no dummy, you know."

"What do you mean?"

"They seemed like the nosy type to me. I didn't want them to get to wondering why you weren't writing anymore, so I mailed them the letter I found in your room. One where you told them how glad you were not to be with them?"

I inhaled sharply, trying to remember what I'd written. All

I knew was that it was angry and horrible and Samantha Rose had won.

"You think those uppity people would want you back? They gave you up quick enough."

"That's not true." I didn't know the particulars, but I knew better than to believe Samantha Rose.

"It is, too." Her face was flushed with anger. "I had to watch Ronelda flit around here like she was better than me my whole life, and now you think you're gonna do it? Ha! If it weren't for me, you'd be with those stuck-up people right now."

"What do you mean?" I asked.

"Who do you think told your daddy's people Ro was putting you up for adoption? They were none too happy to find out Jud's baby was going off the mountain. 'Specially since he was dead and buried."

"You told them?"

"That's right. Ro was acting like you were gonna be some fairy-tale princess or something. Why should her kid be all that while mine was stuck here? She always was selfish!"

I felt dizzy. I was being hit with so much information. My letter had never been mailed. Samantha Rose was the one who got the adoption stopped.

It was all because of Samantha Rose. Everything suddenly made sense.

"You? You stopped the adoption?"

"Ain't that what I just said? Of course, Ronelda threw a

conniption and got you back. Still, a trailer park in Farley wasn't exactly a princess fairy tale, now was it?"

I stood up and walked closer to her. She could have reached out and smacked me or grabbed my ear again, but I wasn't afraid. I wasn't even angry. I was just tired of it all.

I stared her straight in the eye. "Thank you," I said softly, then again, louder. "Thank you! If it weren't for you, I'd never have known my mama." Then I picked up my backpack and shoved my way past.

CHAPTER THIRTY-TWO

If Mr. Vic noticed the bus was quieter than usual the next morning, he didn't mention it. I stared out the window, silent. Camille and Gilbert stared at me.

"I'm sorry, Wavie," Gilbert said for the third time. "I didn't want you to go, but I did, for you. You know what I mean?"

I nodded.

"What time is your hearing tomorrow?" Camille asked.

"One."

"My mom is bringing me. Gilbert and Gran and Mrs. Barnes are coming, too. If you want to tell Mrs. Chipman you'd rather have a foster home, we'll back you up."

"No," I said. "I'll just avoid Samantha Rose for the next seven years until I can leave."

"And her with all your money," Gilbert said. "It ain't right."

I leaned my head on the window and wiped my nose with the bottom of my T-shirt. "Samantha Rose wins."

"Where's the Bowmans' letter?" Gilbert asked. "The last one."

"In my backpack. At least Samantha Rose didn't find that when she searched my room."

"Can I see it?" he asked.

I nodded and passed the letter over. He could keep it, burn it, turn it into an airplane and throw it at Punk for all I cared. The Bowmans were no more family to me than Mr. Vic and they never would be.

I WAS SUPPOSED to be studying for my upcoming Math test, but in the face of Samantha Rose's T-R-E-A-C-H-E-R-Y—CHEATER, HATE, TEAR—I gave myself permission to sulk.

Mrs. Crowder got up from her desk to write more practice problems on the board. While her back was turned, I pulled out the list Mama had given me before she died. The first two were done, over, finished, but that left five to do.

3. The chaplain said since I'm a believer, you and I would meet in heaven if you act right. I told him if it depended on how we acted it'd be a right lonely place. Just 'cause someone's in charge don't mean they're smart. Think for yourself. Also, be good. It doesn't hurt to cover all your bases.

4. No dropping out of school! I'm banking on you being the first Conley to ever go to college. U-N-I-V-E-R-S-I-T-Y even has some fine words in it like NURSE and VET!

5. Cry when you need to but don't dwell. It won't bring me back and you've got to get on with living.
6. Be brave, Wavie B.! You got as much right to a good life as anybody, so find it!
7. Never, ever forget that I loved being your mama more than anything in this big, wide world.

So in a nutshell, be good, stay in school, be happy, think for myself, be brave, remember she loved me. The thing was, right now I didn't want to be good. I wanted to be mean like Hoyt and Samantha Rose, the people who got to do what they wanted.

I had hoped that Mama wouldn't die, but she had. I'd hoped that the Bowmans would write back, but Samantha Rose had nixed that. I could think for myself, and I could see that life wasn't like math, where there was only one answer and if you did the right figuring you'd find it. Life was like science where you gave it your best hypothesis and then through trial and error you either cured a disease or blew up in a lab explosion, and so far I hadn't cured a disease.

The speaker in our classroom squawked. "Mrs. Crowder? Could you send Wavie Conley to the principal's office?"

Mrs. Crowder motioned for me to stand. "She's on her way."

"What'd you do?" Punk Masters whispered.

I shook my head. "I don't know." Other than skipping school with Gilbert that once, I hadn't missed a day.

The office was on the same hallway, just a few feet away from our classroom, but it felt like a mile. By the time I walked to the end and opened the door that read P-R-I-N-C-I-P-A-L (PANIC, PAIN, RIP), my heart was pounding.

Mrs. Rivers smiled from behind her desk. "C'mon in and sit down, Wavie."

I pulled out a chair. "Is something wrong?"

"That was going to be my question to you. How are you settling into life at Farley Middle School?"

"Fine, I guess," I said. "It's not real different from where I was before."

"I see." She looked at me over the top of her glasses. "I've been talking to your teachers."

"You have?"

"Yes. They say that your grades are fine, but that you've become less engaged lately."

"Oh." I clasped my hands together. "I guess I've been distracted."

She sighed. "How are things at home? I imagine life with Samantha Rose could be difficult."

I couldn't help but snort. "Fractions are difficult. Samantha Rose is a whole level of math that hasn't been discovered yet."

Her mouth twitched. "Can the school help? I know you're signed up for the food program. My church gets donated clothes from time to time. Do you need anything like that?"

I shook my head. "I'll be all right. Mama said that a hard life makes people hard." I gave a small smile. "At this rate I'll be a statue by the time I graduate."

Mrs. Rivers looked sad. "Hard living makes hard people sometimes, but it can also make them strong, Wavie. And it doesn't have to make them mean."

I thought of Mama, and Samantha Rose and Hap Conley. "How do you get one and not the other?" I asked.

She held her hand out over the desk, open, and waited until I placed mine inside hers. "You find a reason to keep hoping, Wavie. And an education is a great way to keep hope alive."

"I'll try," I whispered. It was the best I could do.

AS I WALKED up the front steps after school, a burst of color caught my eye. My mother's peony plant had finally started to bloom. I smiled at the tiny pink buds. Mama had said peonies were fickle, so I'd been afraid the plant wouldn't make it, but here it was, blossoming. I might have more of her talent than I knew. Mrs. Rivers had said that education was the key to keeping hope alive. Maybe I'd get some botany books from the library. U-N-I-V-E-R-S-I-T-Y had IVY, VINE and IRIS in it, too.

I bent down to pick a black-eyed Susan. Samantha Rose might be hard like Hap, but I had my grandmother's and my mom's talent for flowers, and no matter what happened, she couldn't take that away.

CHAPTER THIRTY-THREE

"I'm going to the car!" Samantha Rose yelled from the kitchen. "Don't make me come get you."

I walked slowly down the hallway. In a few hours, it would be official and Samantha Rose would be my guardian. I softly tapped the photos of Mama as I walked by. The picture of the two sisters in their Christmas dresses was crooked and I pulled the corner down to straighten it.

"I do look like you," I whispered. "And I'm glad Samantha Rose doesn't." I kissed my fingertip, then placed it on Mama's face. "She's right. You got the best of everything."

The photo of Hap Conley and Marley Savage was crooked but I didn't bother to straighten it. Let the old, mean cuss hang sideways for all I cared. I'd forgotten to give Gilbert the article about Marley that had been taped to the back. I ignored the Buick's horn and retrieved it from my bedroom.

My jeans were stiff from hanging on the line, but at least the dirt had come out. Samantha Rose probably wasn't kidding about returning them once this hearing was over. So far she hadn't noticed my sneakers. I dreaded thinking about what she'd be like once the guardianship was final. G-U-A-R-D-I-A-N-S-H-I-P— GNASH, ANGUISH, PIRANHA.

THE COUNTY COURTHOUSE was only eight miles away, but it was a long, curvy ride. I didn't speak to Samantha Rose once. It didn't matter, because Samantha Rose talked enough for both of us. She talked about how Hoyt wasn't getting to play enough and that coach was going to hear it from her, and how caring for Uncle Philson was wearing her out, and that she didn't understand why Camille's mama was coming to the hearing, like it was any of her business, and why was she bringing the whole Holler with her. But mostly she talked about what I would get if I even thought about causing a problem at the hearing.

The courthouse was busy with folks walking hurriedly across the glossy floor of the lobby. They all spoke in hushed tones, and a few dragged along faded-looking kids wearing serious expressions.

Camille and Gilbert stood across the lobby beside Mrs. Rodriguez, Gran and Mrs. Barnes. They were far enough that Samantha Rose could pretend they weren't there, but I was glad they'd come. Their necks swiveled back and forth as they watched people arrive. Gilbert looked even more nervous than I was.

Mrs. Chipman appeared and explained what was going to happen. "There are several cases to be heard," she said. "If y'all want to come in you can, or I'll come get you when it's time."

"Later," I said. "I don't want to go in yet."

She gave my shoulder a quick squeeze. "Are you okay?"

"Yes, ma'am," I whispered.

"There's nothing to it," she said. "The judge will ask a couple of questions and you'll be back home in time for *Wheel of Fortune*." She gave me a cheery wave and disappeared back inside.

I sighed. Grown-ups almost always saw what they wanted to see. My palms were sweating and I wiped them down my jeans. Something was in my front pocket and I pulled out the newspaper article about Marley Savage.

I walked over to Gilbert and my friends. "Here," I said to Gilbert.

"What's this?" he asked. He was twitching like he'd drunk some of his gran's black coffee.

"I found it while I was cleaning. I forgot to give it to you, but I thought you'd want it since you're looking for Marley's bones and all."

Gilbert barely glanced at it. "Cool. Thanks."

"What is wrong with you?" I whispered. "I'm the one going before the judge."

"Nothing," he said. "I just don't like courtrooms."

Camille grabbed my arm and pointed down the hallway. "Hey," she said, "is that who I think it is?"

Sitting on a bench at the other end of the lobby was a very tall, very thin man wearing a suit. His hair was shorter, and he didn't have a beard, but there was no doubt that it was Angel Davis. An attorney in a business suit and heels sat next to him, talking into her phone.

"What is he doing here?" Samantha Rose hissed.

Mrs. Rodriguez frowned. "He's here for his competency hearing, yes? Didn't you call and turn him in?"

Samantha Rose put her hands on her hips. "That's what concerned neighbors do."

Gran snorted. "I've heard you called a lot of things through the years, Samantha Rose, but concerned ain't one of them."

Angel looked like me, like he'd rather be anywhere but here. I headed toward him.

"Where are you going?" Samantha Rose whispered.

I kept walking. Camille and Gilbert fell in step behind me.

The woman moved her briefcase out of our way and gave us a hard stare but we ignored her. "Hi Angel," I said.

He looked back at us, confused. "What?"

"It's me, Wavie," I said. "Spring beauty?"

Angel's lips curved into a small smile. "That's right." He looked past us to Samantha Rose. "She here to say I'm crazy?"

I shook my head. "No, for me. I'm sorry she called and turned you in."

"I was a lawyer once."

His eyes were weak and watery, and his face was pink from where the beard had kept the sun off his skin. He looked a lot less scary.

Samantha Rose glared at us from across the lobby and waved us back. I turned my shoulders so I wouldn't have to see her.

Angel's shoulders slumped. "I tried to help people, I did." He looked toward Samantha Rose. "I helped her sister but not her."

"That's right. You helped my mama."

"I promised her daddy the girls would stay together." He looked at me. "I did try! But *your* daddy wanted to keep her."

I patted his shoulder. "It's okay."

"It's not okay," he said, his voice rising.

The sharp-eyed attorney glared at us. "Shhhh."

Angel shook his head. "I should have told Hap that he couldn't have her. But he was so mean." He looked at me and whispered, "Your daddy was a bad man."

"I've heard that." I glared at Samantha Rose. "She's just like him."

"Well, her daddy was a nice one—poor old Marley. I wish I hadn't let him down."

I frowned at Gilbert. This was another conversation that was going in circles.

Angel focused on Samantha Rose again. "You don't have to always be so mean!" he yelled at her. His voiced echoed off the marble floors.

The attorney put her phone in her purse and looked at him. "That's enough. When we go inside, you have to stay calm."

"If they let him go home, we can help him," Gilbert said. "In Convict Holler, that is."

Camille nodded and the attorney smiled like we were toddlers being cute. "I'm sure you will."

Mrs. Chipman opened the door and waved to us. "We'll be going in front of the judge soon. Come on in."

Camille and Gilbert exchanged looks.

"What?" I whispered.

"We'll see you inside in a second," Camille said.

Samantha Rose and the rest of the ladies had already moved to follow Mrs. Chipman inside. I looked at Camille and Gilbert, confused. "You're not coming?" I asked, but they were already closing the door. I didn't think I could feel any worse or be any more scared, but apparently I could.

Mrs. Chipman led the way down the aisle and we squeezed together on a wooden bench.

The minutes ticked by and with every one of them, my heart sank a little lower. Finally, the judge rapped his gavel on the podium. "Next!"

Mrs. Chipman stood and walked to the front.

"Your Honor, we're here today to establish guardianship for a minor child, Wavie Boncil Conley," Mrs. Chipman said.

I heard the doors at the back of the courtroom open and a low murmuring.

A voice yelled from the back, "Stop!"

The judge scowled and leaned in his chair to look past Mrs. Chipman.

Turning to look back across the rows, I craned my neck to get a better view. I thought I caught the top of Camille's head. Everyone near us swung around and stared at the back of the room.

"Sit down," Samantha Rose whispered. She pulled the back of my T-shirt, but I jerked away from her.

Camille and Gilbert were standing in the back of the room. Next to them, wearing nervous smiles, were two people I'd only seen in worn photographs but had thought about every day for months. They were a little older, but I'd have recognized them anywhere—Anita and John Bowman.

CHAPTER THIRTY-FOUR

I'd never been inside a judge's chambers. In fact, until the moment I'd been asked to join Judge Harders in his, I didn't even know there was such a thing. I sat on his black leather couch between Camille and Gilbert and tried very hard not to stare at the Bowmans. It was hard to do because they were seriously shiny.

After Gilbert's outburst, everyone had tried to get the story at once. These people were who? They adopted who and when? Gilbert had done what?

I still couldn't believe it. I leaned into him with my shoulder. "You really called them?" I whispered.

Gilbert nodded. "Yep! Turns out they figured it was you who was writing all along. They were trying to take it slow, to give you space. I told them they were about to be a day late and a dollar short."

"These people can't barge in here expecting to get my niece!" Samantha Rose yelled. "It's outrageous!"

Judge Harders banged his desk with his hand. "I need everyone to be quiet!" He pointed to Samantha Rose. "Ma'am, in five words or less, please tell me who you are."

Samantha Rose held up a finger with each word that she spat. "I'm. The. Aunt. Wants. Guardianship." She glared at the Bowmans.

The judge pointed to John Bowman. "And who are you?"

John Bowman smiled at me. "My wife and I attempted to adopt Wavie as an infant."

"Hey!" Samantha Rose yelled. "That's more than five words."

The judge shook his head. "If you can't control yourself, you'll be asked to leave. Now, please continue as *succinctly* as possible."

Mr. Bowman put his arm around his wife. "Our adoption with Wavie was rescinded years ago. Now that Wavie's mother has passed away, we'd like to begin the process again."

The judge looked surprised.

Samantha Rose looked mad enough to spit.

"That was eleven years ago," she said, seething. "They got no claim now!"

The judge leaned back. "In all my years on the bench, this is a first." He looked toward Mrs. Chipman. "Is there a claim? Has an application for guardianship been filed?"

"Just the one," she answered. "That I know of."

"We just learned about the situation this morning," Mr. Bowman said. "We downloaded the application and filled it out in the car." He pulled a folded sheet of paper out of his suit jacket pocket and passed it to the judge.

"It doesn't matter what they have!" Samantha Rose shouted. "You can't break up a family. I'll sue!"

I listened to the adults talk back and forth about me and tried to shake the feeling that, no matter what, Samantha Rose was going to win. She would find a way to get guardianship or to keep the Bowmans from it.

Judge Harders shifted in his chair. "Let me get this straight. Your adoption was rescinded but you want to try again?"

Anita Bowman nodded. "Yes, Your Honor." She turned to give me a quick smile, then turned back around. "We were Wavie's parents for eight days before we learned that the father's family was contesting the adoption. The attorneys thought they might win, so we agreed with Ronelda that the best thing was to send Wavie back to her mom." Her voice cracked on that last word and John Bowman put his arm around her shoulders.

Gilbert elbowed me in the ribs. "This is better than *Judge Judy*," he whispered.

"Why do I have to keep reminding everybody that that was eleven years ago," Samantha Rose said.

"We know exactly how long ago it was," Anita Bowman snapped. For a small thing she was pretty darn feisty. "There hasn't been a day since that we haven't thought about Wavie." She cleared her throat. "Your Honor, I don't expect people who haven't gone through an adoption to understand, but the second we held Wavie, we became her parents. The day we had to give her up was the hardest day of our lives. I've never seen my husband weep like that before or since." She paused to catch her breath. "For the longest time, I could barely talk about Wavie without crying. Some years ago, I decided to contact Ronelda on Wavie's birthday. We exchanged letters and she allowed us to send a small monetary gift a couple of times a year, on Wavie's birthday and at Christmas."

Gilbert's eyes widened. *Small,* he mouthed to me.

Camille grabbed my hand tighter and leaned forward.

Samantha Rose's face turned even redder. "Your Honor. These folks think money solves everything. Just because I don't have as much as they do doesn't mean they can just barge in here and buy my niece!"

"We weren't trying to buy her," John Bowman said loudly, "we loved her. We cared for Ronelda, too." He shook his head. "She trusted us with Wavie and it might have been the worst day when we gave her back, but those first eight days were the best of our lives." He pulled a handkerchief out of his front pocket and blew his nose.

"Then she should have named you guardians," Samantha Rose said. "But she didn't, and family sticks together."

The judge raised both of his hands. "I think I've heard enough. I need to think for a second." A few seconds later, he turned to Mrs. Chipman. "Did Wavie's mom mention the Bowmans to you?"

Mrs. Chipman shook her head. "I'm sorry, no. But then again she didn't mention Samantha Rose either."

"Hmm. That's unusual."

"Your Honor," Anita Bowman said in a small voice. "Ronelda knew how devastated we were after the adoption fell through. I don't think it would have occurred to her to ask us again after all of that."

The judge sighed. "I appreciate that you and your husband want to intervene, but unless I can find cause, the court tries very hard to place children with willing family members."

Samantha Rose stood tall at the judge's words. I could practically see her grow two inches. She'd won. I was headed back to Convict Holler, where I'd probably stay forever until I was buried between Hap Conley and Alma Savage. If she buried me at all and didn't just make me disappear in the woods like Marley Savage.

Marley Savage.

Hap Conley.

Alma Savage.

Angel Davis.

Everything in Conley Holler was connected.

"Gilbert," I whispered. "Quick! Let me see that newspaper article."

He fished it out of his pocket and handed it to me. Angel kept mentioning Marley Savage.

I stared at the grainy photo. My grandpa had been cropped out, but it was the same picture that was hanging on our wall. The same picture that Samantha Rose had shown me and mixed up which one was her dad. Excited, I read the clipping again: *A fund has been set up for the Savages' two daughters at Farley First Union.*

The truth had been in front of us the whole time. Angel had been trying to tell us.

I bolted to my feet. "Judge?"

Judge Harders motioned me forward. "Yes?"

I cleared my throat. "Mrs. Chipman said that the court tends to favor family in matters like this?"

He nodded. "That's right."

"Well," I said, "what if Samantha Rose wasn't actually family? Would that matter?"

"Liar!" Samantha Rose yelled.

"One more word out of you, ma'am, and I'll have you removed." He turned back to me. "Go on."

"Everything in the Holler is connected. Don't you see?" I turned and smiled at Gilbert and Camille. "We have a cemetery that holds my grandparents' graves, but there are others. Mrs. Savage, for one. She died and left two children. Mr. Savage couldn't take it and ran off." I swallowed and kept talking. "There are pictures at the house of my mom and Samantha Rose. They don't look anything alike, but there's a bunch of pictures of Mr. Savage, too. I had to dust them every day and Samantha Rose looks just like him."

I passed the newspaper clipping to the judge. "You can't tell much from that picture, but there are other clearer ones at the house."

Camille was nodding. "Tell him what Angel kept saying."

I clasped my hands together, fighting my nerves. "Angel Davis, our neighbor, kept yelling at Samantha Rose that he'd promised her daddy he'd take care of her. He said he wasn't supposed to split her and her sister up but that my grandpa made him! We all thought he was crazy, but Samantha Rose must have known. That's why she called the law on him. To get him out of Convict—I mean Conley—Holler!"

Samantha Rose's face was thunderous, but she didn't dare speak.

"It all makes sense now," I said. "My mama didn't lie. I asked her once if she had any siblings and she said no, only that one had died as a toddler." I swallowed hard. "She was telling the truth. Samantha Rose wasn't really her sister."

"I don't understand," the judge said. "Your grandpa made this Angel fellow do what?"

"It was because of the child that died," said a soft voice from the back of the room.

Mrs. Barnes and Gran stood against the wall with Mrs. Rodriguez. I'd been so focused on the Bowmans, I hadn't noticed them follow us into the judge's chamber.

"What's that?" the judge asked. "Who are you?"

Mrs. Barnes looked scared enough to faint, but she squared her shoulders and continued. "I've lived next door to the Conleys since I was a girl. I grew up around Wavie's mom and Samantha Rose."

The judge held the newspaper out. "Did you know this Marley fellow?"

She shook her head. "No. But I remember my mama saying that Mrs. Conley, Ronelda's mother, wasn't ever the same after losing her first little girl, Darlene. If Hap told Angel to give him and his wife one of the Savage girls, he would have."

"Thank you," the judge said. He turned to Samantha Rose. "Is this true? Are you the daughter of Marley Savage?"

Samantha Rose crossed her arms, looking furious. For a

minute, I thought she wasn't going to answer. "Yes!" she finally spat. "And Hap Conley never let me forget it. The old goat kept promising he'd make it official, but once Ronelda was born it was like I didn't rate."

The judge sighed and looked at me. "Young lady, you can have a seat. This may take a while."

Then he started talking really fast about birth certificates and wasn't Angel Davis on the docket for the afternoon and could someone find him now and hadn't Mrs. Chipman better process the Bowmans' application and run a background check just in case.

I sat between Gilbert and Camille and watched. I didn't understand everything they were saying, but I knew what it meant when Samantha Rose finally left in a huff, slamming the door behind her. And I had an inkling that something big had just happened when Anita Bowman knelt in front of me, took my hand into hers and burst into happy tears.

CHAPTER THIRTY-FIVE

"**A**re you sure she's not there?" I asked for the third time. It'd been four months since the day of the hearing, and three months, twenty-five days since I'd left Convict Holler. I flipped the window switch back and forth, sending the window up-down, up-down. Gilbert had written to say Samantha Rose, Hoyt and Uncle Philson had loaded up the Buick and left town a few weeks after the hearing, but I couldn't stop worrying that I'd see her.

John smiled from the driver's seat. "We're sure. She hasn't been seen since she hightailed it out of town."

"Where did she go?"

"Don't worry about Samantha Rose," Anita said. "Last we heard, the whole family had moved in with her sister on the other side of the state."

I wondered if Angel had heard, or if he'd understand that the Savage girls were finally together.

John turned off the highway and onto the dirt road. "Conley Hollow, at last." He looked at his watch. "One hour and forty-eight minutes, door to door. That's not bad."

"Can you stop here for a second?" I flipped the switch again to lower the glass and inhaled. "I'd forgotten how good it smells." I turned my head taking it all in. "It really does look different."

They exchanged smiles. "The pictures didn't do it justice?"

"Not at all!" The dusty road was the same, but the entire neighborhood had been bush-hogged. No more briars and brambles lined the ditches. But the biggest changes were at the top of the hill. All the trash and old junk had been hauled off. Not one rusty old car was left. Even Spotted One was lying outside a fresh new dog kennel. I stared at the house. The porch was reattached and the old warped wood had been replaced. The flowers I'd planted stood out in bright colorful waves against the new siding. "I can't believe it," I said.

Anita laughed. "Do you like it?"

"Oh, yes," I said.

When the Bowmans had first asked if I wanted to fix up the house, I'd been confused. "Why?"

"It's your family home," John had said. "It's in pretty bad shape, but the bones are good. I don't see any reason to let it rot."

"But what would we do with it?"

"Now, that'd be up to you," he said. "We could sell it, or rent it, or just hang on to it until you're older and decide then."

"What about Gilbert and Gran? Or Frank and Baily and their mom? Could I let them live there?"

Anita had smiled at that. In fact, smiling seemed her favorite thing to do. "Absolutely."

It had been helpful, those first awkward weeks of getting to know one another, to have something to focus on. Anita and I had pored over paint colors and light fixtures and John had spread out blueprints on the dining room table. But seeing it finished, in real life, was a whole different story.

The screen door opened, and Frank and Baily ran out, followed by Gilbert and Camille. "She's here!" Gilbert yelled.

Gran, Mrs. Barnes, Mrs. Rodriguez and even Edgar were there. They came outside and stood on the porch, watching as I got out and hugged everybody.

"Can you believe it?" Gilbert said. "Me, living in your house!"

"I know," I said. "Which room did you take?"

Gilbert smiled. "Hoyt's, of course. Frank and Baily are in yours."

"Both of them?"

"They took the billboard wall out. Mrs. Barnes says she's going to put it back if they don't quit fighting."

WE'D KEPT FLIPPER Johnson busy by writing long letters back and forth in the months since I'd left. I knew that Camille's dad might open a second restaurant in Lexington next year, which hopefully meant I'd get to see her some on weekends, and that Gilbert had gotten into the GT classes. Even Frank and Baily had sent me a note with a drawing of their cat. I'd told them about my new school and how John had built window boxes for me to plant so that I could see flowers from every room. And how the Bowmans had already taken me back to visit Andro so I could see Hannah and check on Mama's grave.

"Guess what?" Camille said. "We can start e-mailing each other soon!"

"You're getting computers?"

Gilbert snorted. "Nah, but Camille's daddy talked a bunch of business owners into donating more of them for Technology class. They had a fund-raiser to buy books for the library, too."

"What happened to private school?"

Camille smiled. "I changed my mind. If I left, that'd make Gilbert the smartest kid in the school. His head would get so big it'd probably explode!"

"You mean my smile would be so big it'd explode," Gilbert grumbled.

"I'm glad to see not everything has changed." I pulled a picture out of my pocket and handed it to Gilbert. "Here. Camille said you were missing me."

"Whatever!" He grabbed it out of my hand, took one look and grinned. "Look at you. Haven't been gone three months and already sitting in a fancy canoe like you belong there."

John came around the car and stood next to us. "Wavie says you're quite the fisherman, Gilbert. If I bring my rod next time, will you give me a few pointers?"

Gilbert pulled his shoulders back and stood up straighter. "I guess I could give you a tip or two."

"I'd appreciate it. Nothing like being on the river in the middle of the woods, you know what I mean?"

"That's what I've been trying to tell everybody!" Gilbert

turned to me and whispered, "He may be citified but at least he's playing with a full deck."

Gran yelled for us all to come inside while the biscuits were still warm.

I stood in the kitchen, staring. "This looks like something out of a magazine."

A round wooden table sat in the middle surrounded by real chairs, the kind with cushions for seats, and the beat-up linoleum had been replaced. The cabinets all had doors and there wasn't a dirty dish to be found. Even the refrigerator was new.

Mrs. Barnes smiled. "It's the prettiest kitchen in all of Kentucky if you ask me."

Anita smoothed my hair. "Wavie chose the yellow."

The adults sat in the kitchen, while the rest of us took our plates to the living room and watched cartoons with Frank and Baily on the big television that Samantha Rose had bought with my first check.

"I can't believe she didn't take that with her."

"She would have had to go through my mother first," Camille said.

Gilbert put his plate down on the floor. "I forgot to show you something. Come here."

I followed him to the hallway. Anita had arranged for all the photos of my mom to be sent to us, and the walls were now empty except for one large frame. Gilbert stood in front of it grinning.

It was the front page of the *Farley Gazette*. The headline read

CHAOS ERUPTS AT COUNTY COURTHOUSE, and underneath was a black-and-white photo of Gilbert and Mrs. Chipman.

"It's kind of long," Gilbert said, "but here's the best line: 'Gilbert F. Miller, pictured, was responsible for a dramatic day at the Farley County Courthouse. Due to his actions, a young ward of the state was reunited with her adoptive family after eleven years.'"

"'Young ward'? They didn't even use my name!"

Gilbert grinned. "At least you got mentioned. They forgot Camille totally."

"That's awesome," I said. "Did your mom see it?"

"Are you kidding? We had to send her extra copies 'cause hers was so worn out from carrying it around all the time." He stared at the framed print. "Gran's renting out the trailer to a fellow from the mine," he said softly, "so we'll be able to buy a car and visit her soon."

Anita motioned for me from the kitchen. "You finished?"

I nodded and followed her outside. She opened the trunk and handed me a pot and a small shovel. "Take all the time you need. When you're done, do you want to walk up to the cemetery, then maybe visit with Angel?"

"That'd be great."

She went inside while I knelt on the ground by the steps. It wouldn't take long to get a piece of the peony.

I made a small dent in the dirt around the root. I'd do all the things Mama had hoped I would, not because of a list she'd left behind, but because of the love and hope she'd planted in me for eleven years. I put the shovel into the dirt and cut through the roots, dumping a large portion into the pot beside me.

"C'mon, Wavie!" Gilbert yelled from the backyard. "Train's coming. I got you a rock to throw!"

I stood up and put the pot on the porch steps. It was past blooming season, but one faded blossom remained. The scent of it drifted on the breeze, tickling my nose.

Mama couldn't wait to get out of Conley Holler, but I thought she'd like it now. I looked down the hill toward the river. It didn't just look different, it felt different. I could see that there was always hope in the Holler. Where I ended up wasn't as important as who I ended up with. I didn't have her, and I would feel that *not* forever, but that wasn't the end of my story. WAVIE, CAMILLE, GILBERT, BAILY, FRANK, BOWMAN— I could make all kinds of great words out of those. Words like LOVE, FAMILY, LIFE and LIVING, to name a few. Mama had been right, good friends could be like a family.

"I'm finding it, Mama," I whispered. "I'm making a good life."

The coal train came around the bend, its whistle blowing, and I imagined her smiling, watching me down below. LIVING.

ACKNOWLEDGMENTS

Sitting in front of the computer and writing may be a solitary pursuit, but producing a finished novel is anything but. I am forever grateful to the numerous people who helped this book come to life.

JD, you were a fan of Wavie from the get-go, and your unrelenting optimism and encouragement helped me beyond measure. Thank you, Rachel, for allowing me to be distracted for huge chunks of time without resentment. The two of you are my heart.

To my amazing editor, Nancy Paulsen—Wavie and the folks in the Holler were mere shadows of their current selves until they met you. I am so grateful for your wisdom and guidance. Thank you, Sara LaFleur, Chandra Wohleber and the entire team at Nancy Paulsen Books for your invaluable help. Thanks, Dawn Cooper, for the amazing cover. You captured the Holler perfectly.

Susan Hawk, I still can't believe that you're my agent and friend. This wonderful journey started with you. Thank you for believing in me.

Critique groups are essential and I love mine. Thank you, Kim Zachman, Debbie D'Aurelio, Kevin Springer, Alison Hertz, Kristine Anderson, Danny Schnitzlein, Lela Bridgers, Patti Pruitt and Beth O'Neal for your feedback and your friendship. A special thanks goes to honorary member Valerie Nelan for reading that early first draft and for always being my partner-in-crime at SCBWI functions.

To Sheila and Ed Fortier, thank you for sharing your story so generously with me. Your heart for adoption has been a beautiful thing to witness.

Writing a second book is different from the first, and there were nights I didn't believe I could do it. I woke up every morning praying, "God is faithful," over and over. He was and He is.

Thank you, dear reader, for choosing to spend time with Wavie and the gang. You got as much right to a good life as anybody. Go find it!

PRAISE FOR LISA LEWIS TYRE'S
Last in a Long Line of Rebels

★ "Accomplished debut. . . . Strong secondary characters, including Lou's thrice-divorced flirtatious grandmother, help build the strong sense of small-town community. Tyre masterfully weaves historical details into Lou's discoveries in ways that never feel facile, while deftly and satisfyingly resolving past and present puzzles."

—*Publishers Weekly*, starred review

"Determined to save her home, which has been in her family since before the Civil War, Lou musters her Southern girl pluck and sets out on a quest to find the gold rumored to exist somewhere on the property. Along the way, her family's proverbial skeletons come out of the closet, leaving Lou to wrangle with issues of identity and morality. . . . The rumors of the gold, a found diary, and the arrival of a visitor strangely interested in Lou's house add up to an engaging amateur sleuth story, complete with a satisfying ending."

—*The Bulletin of the Center for Children's Books*

"Middle school readers will gain an appreciation for history and mystery as Lou and her friends attempt to unravel her family's tangled past. . . . As they search for clues, they begin to see how the past is closely linked to the present and that injustice did not stop with the Civil War. The small southern town setting, the engaging characters, the well-developed plot, and the exciting resolution make this a charming coming-of-age debut novel. Diary entries add an authentic historical flavor."

—School Library Connection

"The characters are true to life. . . . In the midst of solving a Civil War–era mystery, Lou and her friends confront racism in their own time. Lou feels deeply and is single-minded in her pursuit of justice. A solid debut novel for middle graders who enjoy a blend of history and mystery."

—School Library Journal

"Excerpts from the diary make this feel like historical fiction; Louise Duncan Mayhew's perspective in the 1860s is an intriguing contrast to Lou's modern narration at the turn of the 21st century. . . . Addresses injustice in plain language that is accessible to young readers who enjoy whodunits."

—Kirkus Reviews

"Finding buried treasure, solving an old family mystery, and righting modern wrongs are a few things that push 12-year-old Louise Mayhew's summer from boring to exciting. . . . Tyre's debut features characters that are believable in their naïveté and sense of invincibility. . . . Should please middle-grade readers looking for a solid story with an intriguing historical connection."

—Booklist